E. VALE

THE GIRL ON THE BUS

A Novel

E. Vale
***

This novel is a work of fiction. All characters, locations, and events in this novel—including the state of Stonebridge, the city of Hollis Ridge, and the town of Shadow Creek—are entirely fictional. Any resemblance to actual places or people is purely coincidental. Other names, characters, and incidents occurring in the work are either the product of the author's imagination or are used fictitiously, as fictional events and incidents involving real persons.

***

ISBN: 979-8-9991223-0-8
Cover concept: Completely by E. Vale
Cover layout and graphic design: Created by E. Vale using Canva.com. The child image was generated using AI and modified to retain its original expression.
Editor: E. Vale

Website: **EValeStories.com**

E. VALE

For requests, contact: evalebook78@gmail.com.

***

"This book is dedicated to the seven-year-old child who was left behind!"

Author's Note

Being left on the school bus has always been one of my less-than-pleasant memories. The trauma I endured has certainly followed me into adulthood. It has shaped some of my persona and private relationships. Writing this book has shown me how hard I have struggled to overcome my past. This is why I need to write *The Girl from the Bus*.

Though Leah's ordeal is fictional, the emotional echoes are real. I have been able to heal during this writing journey and come to understand how this event has shaped my adulthood.

This story touches on abandonment trauma and panic attacks. All characters and events sprang from my imagination—no real person was thrown under this literary bus.

Thanks to my real-life fictional Chemistry, who still supports me and helps me overcome challenges. His encouragement kept me writing until the very end. If a person genuinely supports you, don't ignore that someone could see more in you. Thanks to my Scrivener processor for helping me see the entire story.

Did a book ever help you overcome trauma that you carried? Tell me! Visit me at **EValeStories.com** and hop on my blog post. I would love to hear all about it!

—E. Vale—

***

Table of Contents

***

Getting to Know Leilani

Leilani stood at the bus stop, the sharp hiss of the brakes already getting on her nerves. She'd never liked that sound—too loud, too sudden, like a memory you didn't ask for.

At 27, she had carved out a new life in Hollis Ridge, Stonebridge—a far cry from the town she grew up in. Here, the city buzzed with energy and possibility. There were rooftop bars, hidden brunch spots, and just enough chaos to keep things interesting. Most of all, it didn't feel lonely, not like home used to.

Leilani wore her box braids long; she always rocked two colors, copper brown and maroon—her signature look. Thanks to her five-day-a-week cardio grind, her body was all angles and effort.

She was African American, light-skinned with a warm undertone that reminded people of cinnamon and sun. No freckles, though she secretly thought they would've suited her. Dimples too. She'd even considered getting those little piercing things to fake them, but—nah. Too extra.

Still, on days like this, when the wind flirted with her braids and the city felt like it belonged to her, she didn't need any of that. Leilani was never into looks; it was more important that she wouldn't be forgotten.

Leilani was in a situation where she couldn't afford a car, so she was once again standing at the corner waiting for the 25 to crawl up the block. The sharp hiss of air and metal made her stomach twist up. It wasn't the bus itself—it was what it meant—being left and forgotten and being the only kid still sitting there after everyone else had gone home to people waiting for their safe arrival. Most families would know if loved ones were missing. Some children are so lucky always to be noticed.

She shook the thought loose, tugging her coat tighter against the wind. It was below zero, and she was waiting on this slow-ass bus. Man, I need to get myself a quick ride, she thought.

I was left on the bus over twenty years ago, but it was always fresh on her mind like it happened yesterday. She had grown and had a job with benefits, a man she loved, and just enough money to stay out of debt and live her life. The past didn't care about paychecks or rent payments made on time. No matter what she did, she felt like her past followed.

The little girl followed me on the bus, stared at me in the bathroom mirror, and would curl up on the empty side of the bed when Leilani was alone. The scars of her childhood trauma were still fresh, a constant reminder of something she had not let go of.

She needed to catch the bus to get to work. Most of her extra money went to her man, whom she loved so much. She always took out loans to ensure his care. He always needed something, making it hard to keep up with her car payments. Missing those payments had gotten her car repossessed a few months ago.

She also tried her luck at buying a car from the closest auction. But you know how that goes. She could not keep up with the maintenance because there was always something wrong with a vehicle from the auction. She paid someone to take her three hours away to attend the auction. The car did not last for half a year, so she wasted a little over five thousand dollars.

It's all good, though, because she bounces back quickly. She always kept a job—that was one thing she made sure of. Her biggest hurdle was making sure her man was good, because Lord knows he picks the best time to need some money.

Leilani was pulled out of her thoughts once the bus doors creaked open. Leilani then climbed on, her reflection ghosting across the glass for half a second before it disappeared. The driver barely looked up; he just flicked his hand at the fare-box.

As she slid into a seat near the back, the brakes hissed once more—no longer merely a sound. It became a memory. A door creaked open in her mind, and just like that, she was seven years old again, swinging her legs over the sticky brown vinyl seat, watching the world go by.

*

Back in her hometown, Shadow Creek, the bus rattled to a stop in front of Leilani's house, and her stomach knotted up the way it always did when she got close to home. She looked out the window, expecting to see her mother waiting for her. Her mother was nowhere to be seen, and her wait felt like forever until she noticed the bus hadn't opened its doors.

The driver glanced in his rear-view mirror at the rows of kids, scanning faces. The bus monitor stood by the front, clipboard in hand, eyes flicking from paper to kids, paper to kids. For some reason, it has escaped her mind who should be getting off at this stop.

She thought I didn't see any parents; no kids had stood and stated this was their stop. She glanced at the bus driver, confirming we should keep going, but no child was getting off at this stop.

Leilani sat very still; her small hands folded in her lap. She wanted to say something — to wave, to call out, **"This is me, I'm supposed to get off here!"** *— but her mouth wouldn't open. Her voice was deep down, buried under all the times nobody listened.*

Time felt like it was moving at a snail's pace. She thought she was waiting for hours, but it was less than 3 minutes after the bus rolled past her house.

She watched her house disappear through the window, getting smaller and smaller until it was gone.

The ride stretched, kids hopping off at houses where parents stood waiting, arms open wide, voices calling out names like blessings. She watched every hug, smile, and reunion, trying not to wonder why nobody was waiting for her, and trying to understand if her family loved her as much as other families.

She asked why someone was waiting for the different kids from her school. Is it because they are both seen and heard? What is wrong with me, she thought. Am I not special? Does my family not love me?

One by one, the kids disappeared, until it was just her.

The bus pulled into the yard where all the empty buses slept for the night. The engine sighed, the doors hissed open, and the driver stepped off without looking back.

Leilani stayed where she was, too scared to move, too small to be seen. She remembered the yard feeling quiet, isolated, and dark.

The silence felt heavier than the bus itself. And the darkness remained, a stark reminder that she was abandoned by the people who were supposed to protect her. Did they even notice that she was missing? Her heart ached with pain and sadness as the dark environment convinced her that she was now a part of the background. She faded into the darkness, as if she had always belonged. No one had noticed she was missing; maybe she was an imaginary character.

She didn't know how much time passed — minutes, maybe hours — before she saw a flashlight cutting through the dark. The footsteps came next, slow and searching, until they stopped just outside the door.

"Leilani?" a soft voice called. "You on here, baby?" Her voice felt like a stranger's when it finally crept out.

"Yes, I'm here." The doors creaked open again, and someone was looking for her for the first time all day.

The next morning, her mother explained that she had lost track of time and was sorry. She said, "Lani, Momma is so sad, baby. I called you off from school today so *you can take the time to feel better. It will be good for you to take the time and get your mindset in a better place.*

She tried to cheer her up by making her favorite meal, fried chicken, baked macaroni, and white cheese. She also made her favorite dessert, caramel cake, to cheer her up.

Leilani often remembers this day, but the good food did not cheer her up. All she remembers feeling is that the whole situation made her feel like she had no family, and her mother did not love her. Her mother has six kids, including her, and she was used to being completely ignored. She tolerated this because she assumed she was dismissed, but her whole life changed once that bus passed her house without being noticed. She will be forever marked as the child left on the bus, which made her feel ignored.

Later that evening, the bus monitor came to Leilani's house. She knocked on the door, and Leilani's mother answered. Hi, I'm Ms. Holloway, and I was the bus monitor on call yesterday when this unfortunate incident occurred with Leilani. I wanted to come by and apologize for the mistake that happened yesterday. She is such an amazing little girl who doesn't talk much. This was my error as I should have known her stop."

"This is also my fault, I let the time get away from me, and I was not outside waiting." Leilani's mother stated, I have been trying to make it up to her with no such luck. I don't know how long she will take this out on me."

"I have brought her some snacks and clothes, Ms. Holloway stated. "I know this won't make up for anything, but it's the least I can do. I cannot believe that I left that sweet, innocent child. She must think I am a horrible person."

"Yes, of course, let me get her for you. This could help me cheer her up and tell her she is loved," says Leilani's Mother. "I do feel horrible about this."

Leilani is upstairs alone in her room, thinking and staring at the walls. She is still trying to understand what is wrong with her and why her mom would not be waiting for her.

Breaking her from her thoughts, she hears her mom calling her name. She hurriedly jumps up to see why her mother is calling her from downstairs. She knows better than to keep her mother waiting. She also feels like her mom is upset with her due to yesterday's activities.

She thought I should have said something when I was on the bus. I must have embarrassed her. Leilani thought to herself.

Once she reaches the front door, where her mother is, she sees the bus monitor, Ms. Holloway. She is curious, asking herself what she is doing here. Was she in trouble? She thought. Did Ms. Holloway want to yell at her for not saying anything when the bus pulled up at her home? I knew I should have said something when I saw my house. This is all my fault, she thought.

"Hi, how are you doing today, Leilani?" asked Ms. Holloway.

"Hi", she stated, "I'm doing fine. Is everything alright? Did I do something wrong? she asked. She needed to understand why she was here.

"Yes, everything is fine, and no, you did nothing wrong. I wanted to stop by and tell you how sorry I am for what happened yesterday. That was not my intention, and I must do a better job of making sure I am paying attention to all the children riding the bus." She looked at her with so much sincerity.

"I want you to know you did nothing wrong, and everything that happened was my fault. I don't want you thinking anything other than that. I also brought you some snacks and new clothes. I know this solves nothing, but I would like to give these to you as a form of apology. You don't have to accept these gifts, but I want you to know I am truly sorry. No child should ever be left behind or taken to a dark parking lot."

Leilani looked at Ms. Holloway and then looked at her mother. She thought, is she trying to buy me like my mom? Giving gifts to someone you forgot on the bus is a bit awkward. Do they both think food and clothes will make me forget how no one thought of me? What did I do wrong to be put in this situation? She must have gotten lost in her thoughts because she heard her mom call her name. This quickly took her out of her thoughts and made her alert.

"Oh, sorry, Ms. Holloway, I will accept your gifts". She thanked her as she reached over to take the gifts.

"You're very welcome, and I promise to do my job better," she stated with a smile.

Leilani did not know what else to say, so she turned around to leave, leaving her mother and Ms. Holloway to continue their conversation. She did what she did best: shrank into whatever material was close, like no one knew she existed. Sitting in her room, she continued to stare at the walls, her mind filled with a multitude of thoughts.

What her mother and Ms. Holloway didn't understand is that their actions don't matter after the fact. She did not care that they wanted to give her gifts and treat her nicely for a day. Leilani was disturbed because this situation was her fault. If she had only spoken up, maybe she would never have been left on the bus at the graveyard.

My mind keeps replaying the scene from the bus graveyard. I remember the sound of the bus door closing after the bus driver had shut it. He went home to his family for the night. The darkness was so heavy she felt like she was glued to the bus seat and could not move. There were old, grown-out tree limbs that scratched the window. The night's winds made the atmosphere creepier.

Leilani was fading into the background of her bedroom with one final thought on her mind: If I do everything I can to please people, I genuinely believe they **WILL** see me.

Back downstairs, Leilani's mother thanked Ms. Holloway for stopping by. Ms. Holloway provided another sincere apology, promising that such an incident would not happen again. She was genuinely sorry for the pain she caused Leilani. She hopes to mend their relationship and rebuild trust in the future.

This gift, exchanged from Ms. Holloway, continued until the end of elementary school. This began when she was 7, and Ms. Holloway continued the gifts until she completed 5th grade at 10. She had so many new clothes she couldn't wear them all, but she was ready for middle school. She was prepared to move on because, no matter how many snacks or outfits she acquired, Leilani was working on a way to ensure she was always seen.

The bus hit a pothole, jerking Leilani back into the present. She blinked, the memory dissolving into the cracked floor beneath her feet.

That time in her life still haunts her. This memory remains in her mind forever, no matter how happy she feels at the moment. Leilani feels like she is still waiting to be claimed. She loved her man, but sometimes, he tested her patience. No matter what, she will do everything in her power to keep them strong.

As the bus continued, Leilani's thoughts drifted to adulthood, where the haunting memories of her past still lingered. The echoes of her childhood silence and neglect have followed her into her current life, shaping her actions and reactions.

*

Adulthood: The Haunting Memories

Leilani was chillin at her crib listening to Marquise go on and on.

"Lei, I told you I have some big shit in the work. Soon, you won't have to worry about anything. I will bring in more money, and then we can do it.

"Oh, you going to do it big bae? You know if nobody believes you, I do. I got your back, I know you're going to make it happen." She rolled her eyes because this is just him talking.

So often, he has big ideas about making more money. This has been a conversation since we met. I have always made more money than he has. He really could not keep a job, so this is normal. So, I hype him up. He is my man; he will make it big one day because I believe in him.

She didn't argue when he left.

She could have — should have — but the words never reached her throat like they didn't when the bus doors closed all those years ago.

He stood by the door, keys in his hand, smelling like her favorite cologne. She knew what that meant—had known for weeks. But all she did was sit on the edge of the couch, arms crossed tight over her stomach, and nod like it was nothing.

"Alright, Lei. I'm gone. I will head out for a bit to make some moves. I will be back later," he said, already halfway out.

The door clicked shut, and Leilani stayed exactly where she was, staring at the space where he'd been. I wondered why he was always on the move. She does everything for him, keeps a roof over his head, food in the house, and gas in his car. You would think he loves being with me, but he runs out of here whenever I'm off work.

The silence wrapped around her shoulders, heavier than the blanket she kept folded on the couch.

She was again seven in her small hometown in Shadow Creek, Stonebridge.

Leilani was sitting on that bus. Quiet. Small. Pressed against the window, her breath fogging up the glass as she traced patterns only, she would see. The world outside kept moving, cars rushing past, headlights cutting through the dimming light, people walking, talking, laughing. But inside, she was still—a ghost among the living.

She didn't fidget. Didn't tap her foot. Didn't speak. Because speaking didn't matter. No one would turn their head if she whispered, called out, or screamed. No one would see her. The driver stared straight ahead, never checking the mirror. The kids around her filled the space with their voices, jokes, and lives. The bus monitor walks back and forth down the aisle, but Leilani looks at herself in the bus window and sees herself already outside the bus. She watches the bus drive by because she will always be waiting for her loved ones.

The bus rumbled forward, and the streets blurred past, taking her farther from anywhere she belonged. Every stop, every open door, was for someone else. Names were called. Goodbyes were shouted. Friends ran off in pairs. She stayed. She waited because waiting was all she knew how to do.

Nobody was coming for her then. Nobody was stopping for her now. The world kept moving while she continued to wait.

She stood up, pacing the length of the small apartment — seven steps from the window to the kitchen, seven steps back — her heart beating that slow, familiar rhythm: **Don't be seen. Don't take up space. Don't get left.**

Her phone buzzed.

Leilani didn't need to look to know it wasn't him.

It never was. Instead, the screen lit up with a text from her boss: "Be in early tomorrow. I need you to finish up the reports before the client calls." There was no greeting, no explanation, just another demand, another task dumped on her plate.

She exhaled through her nose, tightening her grip on the phone. **No mention of the hours she'd already put in. No acknowledgment that this was his work, not hers.** She was just the unseen force behind every polished presentation, every seamless project, every last-minute fix that made *him* look good. And when the deals closed, when the bonuses rolled in, it was his name that mattered. Not hers.

Her jaw clenched as a sharp and unwelcome memory of her boss's character was put on full display.

****

Leilani sat at her desk, her fingers flying over the keyboard, updating the final proposal for the next big project. She double-checked the numbers, refined the wording, and ensured every slide was perfect, just like she had for the last one.

And just like last time, she knew her boss would take all the credit.

At the post-presentation meeting, Mr. Taylor, one of the executives, noticed a consistent pattern for every meeting. He saw how she clenched her jaw when her boss joked about how "his late nights were paying off." He noticed how she lowered her gaze when the department heads praised him for the seamless execution.

She never spoke up—not this time, not ever! But Mr. Taylor was becoming more noticeable; she rarely paid the higher-ups' attention. However, Mr. Taylor stood out to Leilani, and he was starting to pique her interest.

This was the routine at every meeting she prepared for her boss, Mr. Hardling: every spreadsheet, proposal, and contingency plan was hers.

The late nights, the cold coffee, the weekends spent huddled over her laptop instead of having a life. The project had consumed her, piece by piece, until she had willed it into perfection.

And when the big meeting came—when the department heads sat around that sleek, polished table, eyes sharp with scrutiny—she was ready.

But he was the one who stood at the front of the room.

Clicking through her slides.

Reciting her words.

Taking credit for her vision.

"As you all know, this project was a massive undertaking," he began, shaking his head with a practiced, modest chuckle. "It wasn't easy. There were nights I barely slept, running through the numbers, fine-tuning the logistics. But I knew we could make this happen if I pushed myself hard."

Leilani sat there, her stomach twisting into knots, nails pressing into her palm.

Put in the work?

He hadn't even read the final proposal until twenty minutes before this meeting.

A few executives nodded along, impressed.
"And the data restructuring? That was a beast," he continued, shaking his head. "I must have rewritten the models a dozen times before I finally got it right."

Leilani's fingers curled into a fist under the table.

He rewrote them?

The only thing he had done was forward her emails at the last minute with vague one-liners: "Make it stronger." "Clean this up." "Need this now."

Her heart pounded. It was one thing to omit her name. But to stand there and lie—to rewrite history in real-time, shaping it in his favor—was almost impressive in a sick, twisted way.

Then came the worst part.

An executive asked how the logistics were adjusted and the reason for the change.

Leilani looked up at Mr. Hardling, waiting for him to respond. Before this meeting, she had asked him a million times to check her proposal on why she chose to adjust the logistics.

Mr. Hardling started to stammer. "Well, his voice faded off when I looked over the projections.

"Actually," she started, keeping her voice even, controlled, professional, "the logistics for that were adjusted after the initial report—"

A slow, deliberate chuckle.

A hand raised, silencing her before she could finish.

Leilani," he said, his voice warm, condescending. "I think you might be getting ahead of yourself. Don't worry; I have this explanation. I will get them on the same page about why I made the change."

Then, turning back to the executives, he flashed his signature easy smile.

"She's great with the details. Keeps everything running smoothly. However, I understood that the initial report did not align with the current logistics. This is how I came up with the decision to adjust the logistics."

The executives barely glanced at her, nodding in agreement.

All except one.

Across the table, Mr. Taylor leaned back in his chair, watching her.

Not her boss. Her.

Something flickered in his gaze—subtle, but sharp.

Because he had seen it before.

Her shoulders tensed. Her inhalation through her nose was slow and measured. She smoothed her hands over her skirt, grounding herself.

The way her expression gave away everything before she wiped it clean again.

She was the architect—the real mind behind the work. And yet, here she was, being reduced to a footnote in her success story.

His gaze flickered back to her boss. The man spoke with such confidence and effortless charisma that it seemed he had lived in this project's trenches instead of watching from the sidelines.

Mr. Taylor smirked to himself, but it wasn't amusement—it was understanding. This was what men like him did. Make themselves look good at the other's expense. I am hip to his move and believe I have some ideas.

Steal the credit. Bask in the spotlight. Act like the world's weight had been on their shoulders when, in reality, they had never carried it.

And Leilani?

She was holding it still.

By the time the presentation ended, applause filled the room.

For him.

Executives murmured their approval, shaking his hand and congratulating him on a well-done job.

Leilani sat there, silent.

But Mr. Taylor?

He wasn't clapping.

He was watching.

Because now, he knew exactly who had done the work.

And something told him—he wouldn't stay silent about it. Mr. Taylor got up to leave the room before he headed out. He looked at Leilani and stated, "I enjoyed the presentation today. Something tells me you know more information than you speak. I look forward to hearing more from you. I see great potential in you." He smiled and exited the room.

Leilani looked at him, confused, and smiled. She did not understand what he meant by the good presentation. She did not say anything; she just did the work for which her boss took credit.

Leilani didn't think more about it and was over it for the day. She was not going to give her boss any more attention today. Good for him. Another idea was stolen, and more credit was taken. She made sure to avoid him.

Leilani was jolted back to the present, hearing cars pass outside. I just need to relax and get out of my mind. I really need to get myself a friend to drown out the quietness, she thought out loud. The problem is that Marquise takes all my time, and I can't develop anything past a first meet-up.

***

She was true to her word and headed into the kitchen to grab a glass of wine. She needed to just feel mellow so she could relax. Leilani grabbed her favorite glass from the cabinet. It had an LED light so she could change the color to her mood. She picked a powder baby blue light with continuous blinking. She filled it up with her white wine and returned to the couch.

She decided to take a bath to help her relax. She took her wine glass and put it in the freezer. Then, she ran to the bathroom to start running the bath water.

Leilani said out loud, " I need this water to be super-hot. Please soothe me," she said, watching the tub fill. She took off her clothes.

She looked at herself in the mirror and smiled. She was so happy that Marquise left for the night because all she wanted to do was relax and relieve the tension.

Her water had finished, so she put her hand in the water to check the temperature. It was the perfect temperature. "Let me get in before the water cools off," she said. Leilani got in the tub sporting her birthday suit.

She did not wash up until 30 minutes later. Her body was feeling good, proof that she needed this relaxation and didn't even know it.

She washed her body and stepped out of the tub, grabbing her towel so she could dry off. She lathered her body from top to bottom with baby oil and brushed her teeth. "Eww, the wine will taste funny after brushing my teeth," she said out loud.

She put on a lovely nightgown and grabbed her glass, which she had filled with white wine.

Now, sitting by the window, the phone glowing in her palm, bitterness sat thick in her throat. She should have left this job a long time ago, but leaving meant stepping into the unknown. And at least here, in this awful, unacknowledged space, she knew the rules. Allow my boss to take credit, and I will keep my job.

She needed someone to talk to and blow off some steam, but Marquise had made her cute everyone off. I really miss my cousin Mae. I have not talked to her in about a year, so I'm sure she does not want to hear from me. She smiled and thought about the last time she heard from her cousin Maeve.

**

Leilani was frustrated after another long day of work. She curled up on her couch and dialed Maeve's phone number. She needed her best friend right now. Maeve picked up right away, and Leilani just started talking, not taking a breath.

"Man, Mae, I promise if I have to sit through one more meeting where this ass hole. With his bad lining hot breath dry ass swag having. I might just snap the fuck out. This shit is crazy as hell he keeps taking credit for my work. You should see him talking about shit I did. Most of the time, he is not even explaining it right. Like, why invite me to the meeting if I can't add shit."

Mae's laughter boomed through the phone. "Girl, you should have already snapped on his lame ass. But yo ass so professional, and I'm over here dying laughing. Why are you talking about that man like that?

"Cuz I'm so tired of him. All I do is work and make things happen, you would think he would see my hard work. Not make himself look good. Well, try at least, because he sounds like a fool explaining complex method analysis."

"You're so smart, and I love how you think I understand what the hell you're talking about." She laughed! Plus, you need to relax, babe. You always get what you want. It's not going to be like this forever. You are so hard-working, educated, and determined. You know I do admire that shit.

Leilani sighed. "I just want people to see me, you know? You know I want a career as a project manager. I need people to see and understand that I can analyze and manage big projects. It's not helping that he is taking my credit. But that asshole can't take my experience: I can do this."

Mae's voice softened. "They will. And if they don't? We'll make 'em. I'm here for you, always, cuz. Speaking of with you always, where is Marquise lame ass."

Leilani chuckled, tension easing just a little. "Girl, he's gone like always. I'm glad it's quiet and less needy in here for the moment. I miss you, Mae."

"I miss you, too. Now stop stressing. You're that girl, Lani. Never forget it. "As they said their goodbyes, something settled in Leilani. Mae was still Mae—steady, unwavering.

Returning to the present, Leilani thought that no matter how many years had passed, Maeve had always been there, waiting, and always had her back.

Outside, taillights flickered in the distance, red dots dissolving into the night. Kids' voices echoed from the sidewalk, their laughter fading as parents called them inside. One by one, people disappeared—picked up, expected, wanted.

She remained—the last one left.

But she felt deep down that this might change soon. She had a good feeling and was leaning forward for the first time in her life.

*

The Never–Ending To-Do List

Leilani just hopped off the bus and headed towards her work building. She only had to walk down a couple of blocks to get there. It's good that she worked downtown, getting there much earlier than everyone else was easier. She didn't know what it was, but being alone in the office early in the morning was soothing. She could get so much more work done.

As soon as she got to her desk, she removed her gym shoes and put on heels. She then took her laptop out of her bag and logged in so she could start her day. The first thing she did was open her email, and right away, she knew it would be a long day because her inbox was a mess.

Project updates. Stakeholder emails. Her boss handled follow-ups from teams waiting on approvals.

She was already knee-deep in revising the project timeline when Mr. Harding's voice rang out across the office.

"Leilani! Got a sec?"

She sighed and pushed back from her desk, already knowing what was coming.

His office was spacious—bigger than necessary—and covered in framed photos from company events he barely attended.

He didn't even look up as she walked in; he just gestured toward his desk. "Close the door."

Leilani did.

Harding leaned back in his chair, adjusting his tie like *he* was under pressure. "Alright, so, we've got a little situation. The client wants a revised budget breakdown before the end of the day."

Her stomach dropped. "A full breakdown? Today?"

"Yeah. Nothing crazy, just, you know, detailed cost analysis, projected expenses, contingency planning—the usual."

Leilani inhaled sharply. That wasn't "nothing crazy." That was *his job.* She folded her arms. "That's going to take time. I still must finalize the procurement summary for tomorrow's meeting—"

Harding waved a hand. "Push that. This is a priority."

Everything was a priority when he didn't want to do it.

"Besides," he added, smirking, "you're better at this stuff than I. You get all into the details. I'd mess it up."

Leilani clenched her jaw. *And yet, you still get the paycheck for it.*

"What about approvals?" she asked, trying to stay composed. "The numbers have to be reviewed before submission."

"I'll take a quick glance before sending. Just make sure it's solid."

Translation: *You do all the work, and I'll slap my name on it.*

Leilani exhaled slowly, nodding before walking out.

She rubbed her temples at her desk, staring at the screen.

Another late night. Another impossible deadline.

Of course, when the work is done and the reports are generated, do we know who will receive the praise tomorrow?

Mr. Harding would take all the credit. Again.

Sitting at her desk, she braced herself for the next project meeting, swallowing the tight knot in her throat. She just had to get through it—stay small, stay hidden, I don't need to be present to offer my support.

That always worked, even if she didn't love the feeling it gave her. If no one saw her, no one could blame her. No one could disappoint her. No one would decide if she was worth keeping or not.

She had learned this lesson early on: the quieter she was, the less reason they had to leave.

But Harding wasn't going anywhere.

He sat at the head of the conference table, one hand resting casually on the agenda, the other gripping his coffee like he needed it. He looked relaxed, entirely at ease, like he hadn't spent the past three weeks taking every one of her ideas and presenting them as his own.

"So, before we jump in, I just want to highlight the fantastic work our team has been doing," he said smoothly. "Especially on the revised budget breakdown—it took a lot of number crunching, but we got it done ahead of schedule."

Leilani kept her face neutral, but her fingers twitched against the notepad in her lap.

We?

We didn't do anything. And what team is he talking about? I do the work alone.

The executive nodded, flipping through the report—**her** report. "This is solid work. You went above and beyond, Harding."

He chuckled modestly, shaking his head like it was no big deal. "All in a day's work."

Leilani felt her pulse in her throat.

Then Harding took it further.

"And I've been thinking of a way to streamline our forecasting model even more," he continued, casually flipping to the next page of the report—the **exact** method she had outlined in her notes last night. "If we automate these calculations, we can free up time for higher-level analysis."

That was her plan—word for word. You can't make this shit up; he is a scumbag. Leilani's stomach twisted. Her pen pressed hard into the page of her notepad, nearly ripping the paper.

The executive nodded. "I like that. Harding, why don't you take the lead on that and put together a proposal?"

Harding grinned. "Of course. I'll make it happen."

A slow ripple of approval moved through the room. People nodded. They agreed. They saw **him.**

Leilani swallowed.

It wasn't even just the stolen credit anymore.

It was the way he **acted**, like he deserved it. Like the effort she put in didn't give life to the new forecasting plan.

And the worst part? No one in the room even questioned it.

She stared at Harding as he continued talking, laughing, soaking in the praise.

He is laying this ship on thick. He can't fully explain everything I told him, but why am I surprised? It's not like he listens to me.

But something in her was shifting. There is no way I will continue to do his work, and he takes the credit. I am so tired of dealing with him, the long nights working, and the last-minute edits. She wouldn't say anything today, but she did not know how long she could keep quiet.

Soon, he'd see how it feels to be unseen and never heard. Leilani thought something would change; I can feel it in my bones.

She got her things to head out and catch the next bus. Today was another long and trying day. I hope Marquise is not on bullshit today.

**

Leilani had just gotten off the bus and was now headed to her apartment, which was only a few blocks away, so she couldn't complain.

" I need to get a car quickly. This shit is ridiculous. Just getting on and off the bus makes me so down and depressed. Each time, I feel like a small child on the bus. I know I'm not getting dropped off from school, but I can't help but relive that moment.

When the bus comes to my stop, I always anticipate someone waiting for me. No one is there, Leilani. Get off the bus and go home. No one is waiting for you to get off the bus. I always chant this motivation once I get off the bus.

The tension from work still clung to her as she walked through the door. She dropped her bag by the couch, exhaling slowly. Happy to be home in her safe, quiet space. She wasn't expecting much—maybe silence, maybe the usual distance. But then, her phone buzzed.

Marquise.

"Rough day? Come outside."

Her brows lifted. It is rare for him to ask me to come outside. Man, I'm not in the mood. I hope he is not on any other shit.

She stepped onto the porch, the night air cool against her skin.

And there he was, leaning against his car, arms crossed, watching her like he knew everything she wasn't saying.

He held up a bag.

Her favorite dessert. He had brought her some strawberry shortcake.

Her throat tightened, but this time, it wasn't from frustration.

Marquise smirked. "Figured you could use something sweet."

She just looked at him for a moment, searching for the catch. But there wasn't one. Not tonight.

She stepped closer, taking the bag, and he pulled her in, pressing a slow, lingering kiss to her temple.

"Come ride with me," he murmured. "Clear your head. It seems like you could use some fresh air."

And she did.

They drove with the windows down, city lights flickering past, music low, his hand resting warm on her thigh.

Leilani told him about her day and how her boss still takes credit for her work. She also told him how Mr. Taylor had been paying some attention and wondered what his intentions could be. She just figured all the executives would take her boss's side. Hell, they did not know who did the work. All they know is the job is getting done and it's of fantastic quality—all thanks to me.

He let her vent, didn't rush or brush her off. He never interrupted her because he felt she needed to get a lot off her chest. He just drove and listened while she got off all the frustrations from her day.

By the time they returned, the tension in her chest had unraveled. She was happy that Marquise had been there for her and comforted her.

And when he pulled her close, when his lips traced a slow path down her neck, she melted into him without hesitation.

Tonight, he was here.

Tonight, he was hers.

And for once, she didn't have to carry the weight alone.

*

Leilani's Breaking Point

It was the next day, and the warmth of last night had already faded, replaced by the cold slap of reality.

The **electric bill was due again.**

The weight of it sat heavy in her chest, pressing down, draining whatever was left of the happiness she had clung to. It didn't matter how sweet last night was—the bills didn't care about good moments. They didn't care that you had a great night last night with your man. He finally did something for me and didn't ask or rely on me to do anything.

The high was gone.

And just like that, she was back where she always was—staring at a balance she couldn't ignore, wondering if she'd be the only one who cared enough to handle it.

Leilani sat on the edge of the bed, staring at the screen of her phone, eyes scanning numbers that never seemed enough. The bank balance was a joke and never seemed enough—a cruel one. Rent had just cleared, groceries were already stretched thin, and now the lights.

She exhaled sharply, fingers tightening around the phone. A payday loan meant another cycle of debt. An overdraft fee meant a bigger hole to crawl out of. Either way, the math never worked in her favor. But *somehow*, she always found a way to make it work.

For *him*.

The shower ran in the background, steam curling from beneath the bathroom door like a ghost creeping into the room. Marquise always took long showers when he came home late. Like water could rinse off the scent of wherever he'd been. Whoever he'd been with.

She used to ask.

Now? She didn't even flinch when the sheets smelled different. Didn't react when his phone buzzed at odd hours. Didn't bother pretending that whatever excuse he mumbled was meant for *her* to believe.

She *was* tired. Not just *tired*, but the exhaustion pressed into her chest like a weight. The kind that turned hours into blurs and made her wonder how the hell she even got here.

She traced it back, step by step, like counting backward in a free fall.

The first time she covered his half of the rent, convincing herself it was just temporary. *He's going through a rough patch; it's not a big deal.* The time he used her car for the weekend, and left her stranded. *He promised to bring it back; something must've come up.* The time she drained her savings to clear *his* credit card. *I'm just helping him get back on track.* The time she let go of her dreams because his were always more *urgent*.

How had she let this happen? How did this continue for so long? How did she get off track? He always promised to take care of her.

She blinked at the screen, the overdue notice taunting her. She didn't want to take out another payday loan. She had just paid barely for the last one. And do you think he helped me? No, he was too busy making sure his finances were straight while she went deeper and deeper into debt for a man she believed loved her unconditionally.

Outside the bathroom, Marquise's humming slipped through the door, lazy and unbothered. *Not a damn worry in the world.* He had everything—his bills paid, his stomach full, his clothes washed, his ego fed.

Meanwhile, *she* was the one losing sleep.

She was the one sacrificing.

She was the one drowning.

And what did she get in return?

Silence. Lies. A bed that felt colder every night, no matter how close he pulled her.

Her stomach twisted. The weight of it, all of it, pressed into her ribs until she felt like she couldn't breathe. She had given *everything* to a man who didn't even know what it felt like to go without.

And maybe that was the absolute joke.

Because the one thing he had never once feared losing was *her*.

Her stomach flipped when a notification slid across the screen.

Hollis Ridge Savings & Trust Deposit — $1,200.

Not her account. His.

She only had access because he'd made her set it up back when he couldn't figure out how to link direct deposit. She never checked it — that was his money, his business. But the name on the deposit caught her eye.

Joint Household Support - State of StoneBridge.

Her heart stuttered in her chest. What fucking household? Who is this man supporting with my money?

The shower cut off.

Leilani clicked into the transaction history, fingers trembling—grocery bills — not theirs. Pediatrician copays — they didn't have kids. Car insurance for a minivan — she was out here catching the damn bus.

The statements told the story: **Marquise wasn't just living off her. He was living off her to support his real family — a wife and three kids — in a whole different house.**

The bathroom door opened, steam spilling out like secrets set free. Marquise stood there, towel low on his hips, wiping his face.

Leilani stood there watching her man, well, she thought he was. The water was still running down his chest, the same chest she would snuggle up to while his strong hands were wrapped around her to signify comfort. Now, looking at him, all she wanted to do was rip his head off. She wanted to ask him why he had been playing her this whole relationship. I have given him everything, and this is the thanks I get.

"Damn, you look stressed. What's going on out here?" he said, that lazy smile sliding onto his face like it always did when he thought charm could smooth things over. "Come here, baby, Keez gon' make it better."

Her phone was still in her hand. The evidence was still on the screen.

The little girl inside her — the one who sat quietly on the bus, too scared to say anything was there — curled up in her chest, begging her to swallow it down. To let him lie, so that he wouldn't leave.

But Leilani couldn't. Not this time. For some reason, she could not let this go. She didn't care if he would leave her, she wanted fucking answers.

"Naw, I don't want to feel better, and I'm not trying to get a hug right now. Who's paying for a pediatrician, Marquise?" Her voice came out soft but cut the air like a blade. "And you've got three kids. When were you going to tell me this?"

His smile flickered — just for a second — then came back wider. He figured he was smooth and would talk her down like always. "What are you talking about? You stay trippin', man."

She turned the phone around, holding it up like a mirror, reflecting all the dirt he thought would stay buried.

"You went through my stuff?" he said, his tone sharp, offense curling in his voice like she was out of line. "You don't trust me? That's wild, Leilani. After everything I've been through— "Why would you be checking my things?"

She didn't hear the rest because her 7-year-old younger self had taken over.

**

She was seven again. Sitting on the empty bus as it rumbled back to the depot, her little hands clutching her backpack straps. She could see the houses they passed, all the driveways full of cars.

She sat on the bus, still and quiet, and silent. If she had just made a sound, someone would have known she was there, and someone would have ensured she got off at the right stop.

Was she at fault because she didn't say anything? Did she deserve to be let alone because she did not speak up?

Still, she sat there until the bus was dark and empty. Then, she watched as the door was locked and she was left behind. Leilani didn't look back once he walked away to escape the darkness.

She was broken, forgotten, and waiting for someone to come looking for her. She remembers feeling at fault because this happened. After all, she did not speak up. If only I could do more so people can see me. Perhaps if I can find a way to please people, they will always take notice of me. She determined that moving forward, this is what she would do. She would never be forgotten again.

**

"Leilani! Are you hearing me?" Marquise's voice dragged her back, his face in front of hers now, eyes narrowed. "This is old news, Marquise said. Yes, I have a family, but that has nothing to do with you and me. We can still do this; this shit is nothing.

My family dynamics don't even matter to our situation. That's just a responsibility I currently have. You **wanted** to help me, so why would I stop that? You always do. It's not a problem, baby; we can still make this work."

Leilani's breath felt trapped in her chest like she was suffocating under the weight of his words.

This doesn't change anything.

The audacity. The absolute disregard. He looked at her, like she was nothing more than an extension of his convenience.

She should have seen this coming. She *should have* known.

Her fingers trembled as she clenched her fists, nails digging into her palms, grounding herself in the pain to stay present.

Marquise exhaled loudly, rubbing his hands together like this was just another minor inconvenience he had to talk his way out of. "Damn, you are acting real dramatic right now. We can still make this work. I believe we can get through this together.

Her stomach twisted. *Is he fucking serious right now with this bullshit. He can't feel like this is fucking nothing. He dumb as hell I can't believe this asshole right now!*

"You think our relationship is something special, huh?" He laughed, shaking his head like *she* was the one being ridiculous. "You thought it was just you and me? Where do you think I am for weeks at a time? There are times between me being here and at my family's house, how have you not noticed? Well, it's not like you can pay attention to anything because you work overtime. If you ask me, this is a good thing that you know I don't have to be sneaking around."

The words hit like a punch to the gut. Does he think I will agree to this? Does he believe I'm going to accept this nonsense?

All these years, all the sacrifices—*for what*?

Her voice came out hoarse but sharp. "I *gave* you everything."

"And I let you." He shrugged, his eyes cold and empty. Nobody told you to, though. That was *your* choice. You wanted to take care of me, thank you! I owe you a lot, and I'm always here, so if I owe you, you will never be broke," he replied, laughing!

She sucked in a breath. This shit is not funny, and I'm not in the mood to play games.

This man had drained her dry—her love, her money, her energy—and now he sat there, barefaced, telling her none of it matters. That she was a fool for ever believing he did.

She swallowed hard. "So, what now, Marquise? Do you want me to keep paying for your life? Your kids? While you lay up with *her*? While our relationship stays on the same damn level. I wanted to be somebody's wife one day, and now I know you won't be my husband. This is great I have wasted so much of my damn time."

He smirked. "Wait a motherfucking minute. So, you were doing all this work thinking I would give you a title later? Come on, married, how, Lei? We have never talked about that before. How was I supposed to know that marriage was in your future? You're funny, thinking I can read your mind."

Marquise let out a dry, humorless chuckle, shaking his head. "Wow. So now you're the victim? You've been throwing money around like it could buy loyalty and make me love you the way you wanted. Newsflash, Leilani— it doesn't. It never did and it never will."

He lowered his voice a step closer, but the words hit just as hard. "You wanna be somebody's wife? That's cute. But let's be real—you never even knew how to be somebody's woman—always trying to make things right and pay for my mistakes. You are here waiting for me to turn into some perfect man in your little fantasy. That's your problem. You live in your head instead of seeing what's right in front of you."

His lip curled as he shook his head. "You talk about wasted time like I begged you to stay. You made that choice, sweetheart. And now that it didn't turn out how you wanted, you wanna cry about it? That's on you."

He grabbed his keys, turned toward the door, and paused to deliver his final words. "You keep trying to buy people, thinking it'll make you whole. But here's the thing—you were broken before I got here. And it seems like you still are and you need to work through the shit. It's not my job to fix you Leilani so deal with your shit. I've got to make some runs, see you once I get back?"

With that, he walked out, shutting the door behind him.

She paused for half a second, not believing the words he had just spoken to her. He made sure to leave before I could get a word in. He wanted to talk slick, as if this shit was my fault—I'm not the one with the hidden family.

Leilani sat there for a long time; she didn't move. Couldn't. His words echoed in the silence, wrapping around her like chains, suffocating her. Broken. Always trying to buy people, and he feels like I have been broken. Well, tell me how you really feel, motherfucka.

Her knees buckled, and she sank onto the couch, gripping the edge like it could hold her together. Was he right? Had she been fooling herself this whole time? Maybe she had. Perhaps she had spent her entire life chasing love, hoping it would make up for the years she had been left behind. Hoping it would finally mean she was enough.

Tears burned her eyes, but she swallowed them down. No. Not this time.

She had spent so much time waiting for Marquise to change, for someone to choose her, and to feel like she mattered. But what if she stopped waiting? What if, for once, she decided to pick herself?

Her chest rose and fell in uneven breaths as the weight of it all settled. The pain was still there, sharp and unforgiving, but beneath it, something else stirred— something small, fragile, and real.

A quiet voice in her mind whispered: *Maybe it's time to start loving me instead.*

She wiped her face, straightened her back, and took her first deep breath in years.

She exhaled through her nose, her whole body vibrating with anger, with exhaustion, with the sudden, crushing *clarity* that she had wasted so many years on someone who never once saw her as anything more than a resource.

The walls of the bedroom seemed to close in — the same bedroom where she spent countless nights crying while he was "out handling business." The same bed where she lay awake, wondering what she had done wrong, why she couldn't be enough.

And she didn't even know who she was without him. How did she lose herself after all these years?
Was this the end?

Or was this the beginning? The space began to open quietly, and she saw a shadow of faint light. New beginnings were coming, whether she was ready or not.
*

Leilani's Inner Breakdown

It was the next morning, and she still wasn't feeling well. The weight of everything sat heavily on her chest, making it hard to breathe and hard to think. She emailed her boss to call off work, without bothering to check if she got a reply. She then threw her phone somewhere on the nightstand, face down, totally ignoring it, hoping it meant she could ignore reality itself.

The only thing she could think to do was shut herself away. Her room felt like the only place she had control in the world. The door was closed, something she rarely did, and the silence felt suffocating yet safe.

Leilani sat curled on the bed, her body drained from the night before. Her thoughts were tangled—one moment, she felt nothing, just an empty numbness, and the next, a wave of emotions would crash over her, threatening to drag her under.

Then she heard it.

The front door opens and shuts.

Her stomach twisted. **Damn.** She thought she'd have the apartment to herself, space to think, to unravel everything in private. Any other time they argued, Marquise would disappear for a few days, running off to whoever, well, now I know he was running off to his family. But today? He was here.

She sat frozen on the bed, listening.

Marquise was moving around, his footsteps heavy, deliberate. He wanted her to hear him. He wasn't sneaking in like he had something to hide. No, he was making sure she **knew** he was home. The sound of the fridge opening and cabinets closing—he was in the kitchen now, being unnecessarily loud about it.

Her jaw tightened. She wasn't ready for this.

Then came his voice, casual, cocky. **Too cocky.**

"So, you just gon stay locked up in there all day?"

Leilani closed her eyes. He wanted to see her reaction, to see if she was still mad or hurt. She didn't answer.

A slow chuckle. "Oh, we're doing the silent treatment now? That's cute."

She heard his footsteps moving closer, then a light knock on the door. He didn't even wait for her to answer before pushing it open.

Leilani snapped her head toward him. "Did I say you could come in here?"

Marquise leaned against the door-frame, arms crossed, his expression smug. "Since when do I need permission to come in my place?"

She exhaled sharply. **His** place? **His?** As if she hadn't been paying most of the damn bills.

"Funny how you always pull that 'my place' shit when it's convenient," she muttered, rubbing her temples.

He smirked. "You really that mad, huh?"

Leilani shot up from the bed. "Mad?" she scoffed. "Nah, I'm past that. I'm embarrassed. I let you make a fool of me for years. I should be done with everything I have dealt with over the years."

Marquise's smirk faltered for half a second before he caught himself. "That's crazy. 'Cause just last week, you were talkin' 'bout how much you love me." He took a step closer. "That's still true, right?"

She stared at him, disgusted. "You really think I'd still love you after everything? You think I should stand here and play second with you. Waiting for you to come to my house, cause at this point you've got your own home. I can't believe it after everything; this is how you do me."

He shrugged, unbothered. "I think you don't know how to be alone. And I think the second I'm really gone, you gon' realize you need me. I think for you to feel like you matter, you need a living person to care for. You need someone to be responsible for so you can feel complete."

Something inside her snapped.

Leilani let out a bitter laugh. "Need you? The only thing I **need to do** is wake the hell up."

Marquise's expression hardened. "Oh, so now you tryna act brand new? Now, I did something to you, and you had no idea what was happening. I am rarely here Leilani what the fuck did you think was happening."

"New?" She shook her head, stepping closer to him, refusing to shrink under his presence like she used to. "Nah, this is me finally seeing shit for what it is. You don't love me. You like knowing you **could** have me and use me for my funds. And now that I'm not playing along, you don't know what to do with yourself."

His jaw clenched. "You really think that you will be better off without me? You really think you're gonna find half a man like me? Who would want an insecure ass female that's clingy?"

She met his gaze without hesitation. "I **know** I am. And that's the thing; I don't need anybody to take care of me. I have cared for you all these years, so I think I will be fine."

For the first time, Marquise had no comeback. No slick remark. No manipulation wrapped in sweet words. He just stood there, his eyes narrowing slightly, as if trying to decide whether to argue or walk away.

Then, with a scoff, he turned and started walking away. "Aight. Bet." He walked out, slamming the door behind him.

The moment he was gone, the room felt different—lighter.

Leilani sat back on the bed, gripping the sheets as the emotions hit her simultaneously.

She should have been crying, scared, and broken. She knew how it felt to be alone and forgotten about, but she did not care.

She would no longer let that man take advantage of her.

For the first time in a long time, she **wasn't scared to be alone.**

Instead, she felt something else stirring inside her. Something unfamiliar but substantial.

Maybe, just maybe... it was self-respect.

And it felt damn good.

She could have asked him to leave. She should have.

The thought still sent a tremor through her, but it wasn't fear twisting her stomach this time—it was something else. A pull, quiet but steady, like the first warm breeze after a brutal winter.

Because if Marquise was gone... then what?

The silence would be loud, yes. Unfamiliar. But maybe it wasn't a void meant to swallow her whole. Maybe it was space—room to breathe, to exist without shrinking, to hear herself think.

She leaned forward, elbows on her knees, but her hands didn't cradle her head this time. They rested on her thighs, fingers curling slightly, as if bracing for something new.

The memories still came, but they weren't chains anymore— echoes of things she didn't have to carry. The late nights, the empty holidays, the missing pieces she had forced herself to ignore. She saw them all now, clear as day, but she let them drift past instead of drowning in them.

She had known.

And now, she knew something else.
She realized that having someone does not equate to love, especially if that someone is treating her with disrespect. And being needed isn't the same as being wanted.

For the first time in a long time, she wondered what it would feel like to be wanted. To be chosen. Not just by someone else, but by herself.

The thought didn't terrify her.

It felt like the beginning of something.

Something real.

Something hers.

Her fingers trembled as she scrolled through her text messages, looking for someone to talk to — anyone who might ground her back into reality.

She had acquaintances at work who had stopped asking about Marquise months ago, after too many "it's complicated" conversations. She didn't blame them. Even Leilani was tired of her excuses and talking about the same topic.

Her mom? No. Her mom was the first to teach her that **love means swallowing your pain to keep someone else comfortable**.

Leilani rarely talks to her mother because the conversation never goes anywhere. Her mother has a tendency to blame me for my emotions, and my feelings are never valid to her. She is the biggest hater, and I do not have the energy to deal with more negativity today.

She kept scrolling through her contacts and found no one to call.

Panic crept up her throat, and her breaths came shorter. She needed noise—she needed distraction.

She hadn't planned on checking or even realized she was typing until the name filled the search bar like it had been waiting there all along.

Monica Taylor.

The profile popped up instantly, the perfect little family staring back at her.

Matching outfits at Christmas. Sun-kissed smiles on the beach. A video of their baby's first steps, Marquise's deep laugh in the background as he cheered them on.

Leilani's chest tightened, breath hitching. **She paid for this.** Every time she asked for an overtime shift, it was to cover bills at a home she never visited. Time after time, she sacrificed every dollar so Marquise had "what he needed." She wasn't building a life with him. She was funding one for them. For his wife and family's happiness.

Her hands trembled as she scrolled further, past anniversary posts and "#Blessed" captions, until she landed on a photo that sent a sharp, physical pain through her.

Monica is in a hospital bed. Sweat on her brow. A newborn curled against her chest.

And Marquise.

Standing next to her, pressing a kiss to her forehead, fingers laced with hers. Looking at her like she was his world.

Leilani's stomach dropped, nausea clawing its way up her throat. She shut her phone so fast she nearly dropped it onto the floor.

She **knew** what Marquise was. She **knew** she wasn't the only one in his life. But seeing it, **feeling** it, was something else.

She just sat there momentarily, fingers clenched around the phone, heart pounding.

With a clearer mind, she reopened her phone and scrolled through her contacts again. Her thumb hovered for a second before she tapped the name.

**

Maeve.

The phone barely rang twice before a familiar, slightly breathless voice answered.

"Oh my God. **Leilani?**"

A lump formed in her throat at the pure shock in Maeve's tone. "Hey, Maeve."

A beat of silence. Then—

"Girl, are you in jail?"

Despite everything, a laugh bubbled up. "What? Why would that be the first thing you say to me?"

"Well, damn, you ghost me for years, and the first time you call, I had to make sure," Maeve shot back, her voice lighter now, teasing but not unkind. "For real, though. I've been trying to reach you. How are you doing, Leilani?"

Leilani exhaled, her eyes flicking back to her darkened screen. The ghosts of those perfect pictures still burned in her mind.

"I am not doing well, just found out some information I'm unhappy about."

Maeve's voice softened. "What happened?"

Leilani swallowed hard. "I just…" she hesitated, gripping the phone tighter. "I was on Instagram."

A dramatic groan came through the receiver. "First mistake."

Leilani let out a weak laugh. "Yeah, but to be fair, I never knew a Monica. I had no reason to look up that woman's name. This shit has threw me off and now I have no idea what is going on."

"Oh, I think I do," Mae said knowingly. "Go on."

She hesitated, then let it spill out, raw and unfiltered, how she had unconsciously checked Monica's page. She had seen everything—the family trips, the baby, the delivery room photo how she had felt **every ounce** of what she had been feeling for **too damn long.**

When she finished, there was a pause. Then, Mae let out a long, slow breath.

"That attention seeking ass **Bitch.**"
Leilani choked on a laugh, something between a sob and relief.

"Nah, for real," Mae continued. "You out here killing yourself for this man, and he's playing happy husband? He got you skipping out on your own damn life to pay for his?"

Leilani swallowed. "Yeah."

Another silence, this one heavier. Then—

"You're done, right?"

It wasn't a question.

Leilani shut her eyes. "I don't know, it's hard to think about being alone."

"You do," Mae pressed. "You just don't want to say it yet. And who says you will be alone? You don't need him to feel loved."

Leilani opened her mouth, but no words came out.

Mae sighed. "Look, I know you love him and y'all have been together for years. I know you wanted this to mean something. But **you deserve better.**"

Leilani felt something crack inside her— something fragile, something she had been holding together for far too long.

"I just... I need my best friend back," she whispered, voice barely above a breath.

Mae's answer was immediate. **"Girl, you better start answering my calls, then. Don't make me pull up on that ass."** Then, softer, "I missed you too. We are nothing without each other."

Leilani was so happy, and she felt loved all over. It made her deeply happy that this feeling could come from a family member.

They kept talking, the conversation stretching long into the night. For the first time in a long time, she wasn't alone.

Everything has changed between her and Marquise, and it's out of her control now. This is not her mess to clean up, and for the first time, she was gone to see how this plays out.

Once she got off the phone, her mind wandered to one of her favorite memories of her and Mae.

***

The sun blazed overhead, making the pavement sizzle as Leilani and Mae sat on the curb, swinging their legs and wiping sweat from their brows. The faint jingle of an ice cream truck drifted through the air, growing louder as it rolled onto their block.

Leilani perked up. "Ohhh, we gotta get some."

Mae hopped to her feet, already plotting. "Okay, okay—Mama might have some change. Wait right here, I'll go ask."

Before Leilani could answer, Mae took off toward the house, her curls bouncing with each determined step.

Leilani smirked. She already had a better plan.

Across the street, leaning against a beat-up car, was Mae's older brother, Marcus. He was always posted up with his friends, his face unreadable, his world much bigger than theirs. But one thing was sure—no matter what streets he ran, Marcus ensured Mae and Leilani stayed just kids.

Leilani marched up, hands on her hips. "Marcus."

He lifted an eyebrow, amused. "What's up, shorty?"

"The ice cream truck." She pointed at it like it was a matter of life and death. "We need to get some."

Marcus exhaled a small laugh, shaking his head. "Ain't got no money, Leilani."

Leilani squinted at him. "You do. I spent the night, and you were out all night. You got something for me, bro?"

His homeboys started chuckling.

Marcus sighed, reaching into his pocket and pulling a few crumpled bills. "Man, y'all somethin' else." He handed her the cash. "Go on before I change my mind. And stay out of my business, little girl."

Leilani grinned widely. "You're the best, big bro. And don't worry; I ain't seen nothing," she laughed!

She ran back just as the ice cream truck stopped, making her move fast before Mae returned—two soft-serve cones, one for each.

By the time Mae came skipping back, her face had fallen. "Mama said no."

Leilani just smiled, holding out a cone.

Mae blinked. "Wait—what?"

Leilani licked her ice cream, grinning. "You missed it. Big bro got us."

Mae's jaw dropped, and she threw her head back, cackling. "Girl, you play too much!

He didn't come into the house all night, so I'm not surprised he gave up some funds. Shoot, he had better ran those pockets and he was out making money, we're not slow."

Leilani laughed, "I said the same thing he said, stay out of his business."

Mae laughed with her, the sticky ice cream dripping down their fingers as they sat back on the curb— just two kids, with the whole summer ahead and a big brother watching their backs.

Leilani smiled, thinking of her past memories with her favorite cousin. Maybe she had lost time. Perhaps she had lost pieces of herself along the way. But she wasn't lost. Not anymore.

*

Leilani's Spiral Deepens

A few days later, Leilani stood at the kitchen sink, hands plunged into lukewarm, soapy water, scrubbing the same plate for the third time. Her eyes weren't on the plate, though. They were locked on Marquise's keys — sitting on the counter, next to his phone, wallet, and whole life.

A life she paid for.

She knew the contents of that wallet better than her own. She set him up as an authorized credit card user, but don't worry; he uses it freely. The crumpled receipts from places they had never been to were tucked behind his ID. The folded paper with **Monica's number** scribbled in blue ink was tucked behind his ID.

Her hands kept scrubbing even though the plate was already clean.

The sound of the water running filled the silence, but not enough.

Marquise was in the living room, stretched out on **her couch**, rolling a blunt like nothing had happened. Like she hadn't caught him. Like she wasn't sitting there swallowing her screams every time she looked at him.

He was too calm. Too comfortable.

Because she always **made it comfortable** for him.

Leilani's breath hitched in her throat. Her stomach tightened like a fist, but she kept scrubbing, her fingers wrinkling from the water. Her mind drifted back to the bus, the empty seats, and the little girl who didn't say a word when they passed her house.

That silence — it lived inside her still. It had grown up with her. It had followed her into every relationship, every argument she swallowed, every "it's fine," she whispered when it wasn't.

Her hands shook in the water, bubbles sliding down her wrists like tears.

"Lai, you good. Why are you so quiet? You're still not talking to me. You should be calm and collected. Let that shit go. It is what it is." Marquise's voice slid into the kitchen, smooth and careless.

She froze, her heart slamming against her ribs. She wiped her hands on a dish towel, forcing herself to turn around, leaning against the counter to face him.

His eyes were half-lidded, lazy like this was just **another night.**

He was wearing the hoodie she bought him, the socks she stuffed in his drawer, and his phone charger plugged into her outlet.

She couldn't breathe. I'm so tired of this dude just a fucking user no matter what. Looking at him makes me disgusted. He needs to get lost. Why is he even there?

"Naw, I'm not good. I thought I would have some time to myself to think things through," she lied, voice barely there. "Don't you have some runs to make? Maybe you can pick your kids up from daycare. I'm sure there could be so much more you could be doing than sitting in my face, you know, because you have a family and everything."

Marquise sat there looking confused, like he couldn't understand where she was coming from — the **dissatisfaction on his face**. What was she not afraid of losing me? He thought. I'll fix this. I need this bitch who else gone help pay my bills.

He leaned back, stretching. "Lei, come on now, baby. We can get past this. It may seem like you need some time, but it's better if we take this one day at a time. There's no point stressing over this because it's not worth it. I'm still yours, and you're still mine, baby. We're going to make it together."

Get past it? He is a narcissist, thinking everything revolves around him. What an idiot.

Leilani's stomach turned.

Her fingers curled into the damp towel, knuckles white. She stared at him, the man who lay beside her every night while building a life with another woman.

The man who made her **his backup plan**, ATM, and **emotional dumping ground**.

And she let him.

She fucking let him.

The thought crashed into her with so much force that her knees weakened.

Her body was rebelling, her mind splitting — half of her screaming to **say something**, to **stand up for herself**, to **demand her worth**. However, she had no energy for his nonsense today; he just needed to move around. If I weren't in this damn apartment lease, I would have changed the locks.

Her other half wanted to take control—the 7-year-old half—because she was still sitting on the bus, too afraid to speak or be seen. Maybe if I kept quiet, he could leave while I got myself together.

"Leilani?" Marquise's voice cut in again, sharper this time. "You hear me?"

She blinked, realizing she'd zoned out. Her heart was racing. Her mouth was dry.

Yeah," she croaked, stepping away from the counter. "I'm just tired, Marquise, just because you can let things go does not mean I can do the same. I am still dealing with this shit. You knew about your family I fucking did not." She shouted.

"You need to calm the fuck down and watch who you talking to. I understand you're upset, but you need to lower your voice right motherfucking now." He matched her tone.

"I'm not doing shit this my house and if I want to shout in this bitch I will. I don't understand why you're here forcing some shit on me. Is it going to hurt you to give me some damn time. I'm not moving on your time. Not this time."

Leilani walked over to the stove to start frying her naked chicken. She wanted some chicken and smothered potatoes on the side. She made sure to take out just enough for herself to eat. She put just two small potatoes to boil so they could soften up. She was not cooking for his dog ass not today.

"So, you're not cooking for me? I see you take out that little ass chicken and why you boiling just a couple of potatoes. You know I like extra when you make that shit." He asked.

"Marquise, I told you to take yo ass on. I'm not cooking you shit today go home and eat with your family. I am cooking for myself to have a nice, relaxing dinner alone tonight." I can't believe I said that she thought.

"You know yo ass don't like to be alone so you need to stop. If it was any other night, you be in your feelings if I didn't want to eat with yo hard headed ass." Marquise said with a frown.

"Well, guess what tonight is that night," she said while walking into the living room, turning on a movie she wanted to watch, and ending the conversation with him immediately. She sat on the couch, ignoring him, waiting for when she needed to go into the kitchen and check on her food.

Marquise just stood there and watched her in disbelief. "Leilani, you are not going to cook me something to eat?" he asked one final time, frustrated.

Leilani ignored him and turned the volume up slightly. After he stood there for about five minutes, she went and flipped her chicken, then sat back down and enjoyed her movie.

"Man, you tripping." Said Marquise. "I am going to go and let you cool down. Maybe you do need some time to find some sense to ya self. I'm out." He walked over and opened the door. He stood there for a second, thinking she would respond. But she never did; he just closed the door behind him.

Walking to his car, he thought Man, she needs more time. Everything will be fine; she's just trying to show strength in this moment. I will give her this little time. He smiled while pulling off, but she couldn't stay away from him.

Finally, alone in her apartment, Leilani was happy he was gone. She had nothing else to say to him at this moment: "He can't force me to do shit right now. I need a moment to figure out my next move." This is going to happen whether he allows it or not. The ball is not in his court, and if he believes that or not is his problem.

The silence settled over her, but it wasn't empty.

It was **full** — with every memory, every sacrifice, every piece of herself she'd handed over without asking for anything in return.

She had been disappearing for years, piece by piece.

And now, she was almost **gone**.

Tears slipped from the corners of her eyes, but she didn't make a sound.

Because silence was the only language she knew how to speak, she did not know how she would move forward, but she would finally take the time to see.

*

Final Breaking Point

After about a week, the suitcase sat by the door, half-zipped, a pair of Marquise's sneakers hanging out like a tongue. Leilani stood in the kitchen doorway, arms crossed tight against her chest, her fingers digging into her arms to keep her hands from shaking.

Marquise was pacing, cell phone in one hand, blunt tucked behind his ear, eyes flicking to her every few seconds like he was measuring how much work he had left to do to get her back on his side. His voice was smooth and persuasive, the same one that had talked her out of walking away. The one that had kept her in his orbit, no matter how many times he spun off course.

"This trip, baby," he said, his voice thick with fake excitement, "this is it. This is the one that's going to change everything for us."

Us. The word tasted like rust in her mouth.

He turned to her, his face shifting into that perfect balance of urgency and devotion that had once made her feel special and chosen. His hands found her hips, warm and familiar, pulling her close like he hadn't been sleeping in a bed she paid for while sending "good morning, beautiful" texts to another woman.

To his wife.

His thumbs traced slow circles on her waist, trying to smooth out the tension he had placed there, his grip firm but careful, like he knew he was on thin ice. "I'm tellin' you, Lai," he murmured, voice softer now, leaning in like he was about to whisper a secret meant only for her, "this interview is big. Like, life-changing. Corporate-level shit. They're flying me out, putting me up in a nice spot. All expenses paid."

Her silence sat heavy between them, and he took it as a sign to double down.

"And when I get back?" He kissed her forehead, lingering, like he wanted her to feel it and press the lie into her skin. "We're good. I'm able to spoil you the way you deserve. You've been holding me down so long, too long. It's time I hold you down. You're my rib, my everything. And I swear, after this, everything changes. No more sneaking, no more waiting. Just us."

Her heart clenched because it sounded real for a moment, for a dangerous, fleeting moment.

His hands slid up, cupping her face, his eyes locking onto hers like he could see inside her, like he was reading the war waging in her head and knew exactly how to tip the scales in his favor.

"Lei," he said, his voice dropping into something raw, something he didn't use often—something that made her chest ache. "I know the last few weeks have been hell on you. Finding out about... everything. I hurt you. I see it every time I look at you. And I hate myself for it."

She swallowed hard.

"I should have told you the truth from the jump," he continued, thumb brushing over her cheek like he memorized her feel. "But, baby, I swear to God, I never meant to hurt you. I never meant for it to be like this. It was just... it got complicated. And now, I know what I want. I know what I need. And it's you."

Her breath hitched.

"If you just give me time, I'ma fix it. I'm already looking at the divorce process, baby, I swear. You gotta trust me," he pleaded, pressing his forehead against hers. "I just need you to hold me down one more time."

Her body betrayed her, leaning into him, wanting to believe, needing to accept, because what was the alternative? That she had wasted years of her life? That she had built her future around a man who was never really hers?

She shut her eyes. "What about your kids?" Her voice was small, unsure. "Why would you break up your family?"

Marquise exhaled hard, like the weight of it all was crushing him. "That's the hardest part, baby. That's what's been eating me up. But I ain't no good to them like this. Living a lie. Pretending. I gotta do this the right way. For them. For me. For us."

She wanted to believe him. God, she wanted to believe him.

"You mean the world to me," he said, his grip tightening just enough. "I know I was selfish. I know I didn't think about what this would do to you, and that's on me.

But I'm done being careless with your heart, baby. ... don't give up on me yet."

She nodded, slowly and hesitantly. The air between them was thick and sticky, laced with something that felt like a lie left out too long.

Before disappearing, he kissed her, soft, sweet, as always. "We got this, Lai. Just hold me down one more time."

She forced a smile. "You're right, we got this, Marquise."

Marquise grabbed his suitcase, whistling low as he stepped out the door, leaving her in the silence he always left behind.

*

Hours later, Leilani sat curled on the couch, her work laptop open, half-answering emails, half-staring at the walls. The house was too quiet. Too still. Without Marquise's voice filling the space, the silence pressed against her ears like cotton.

She glanced at the door, half-expecting, half-hoping it would swing open and he'd walk back in like none of this was real. She hadn't just let him leave with promises that tasted like honey and arsenic.

Her phone vibrated against the coffee table. The sharp sound jolted her out of her fog.

A text from her cousin Maeve. Just a link. No message.

Leilani frowned and clicked it.

The screen loaded.

And then her world cracked open.

A Facebook post. A smiling Black woman with thick braids cascading over her shoulders and a beautiful pink sun-dress hugging her curves. The caption read:

"Anniversary cruise with my KING & our babies! Twenty years strong & still my everything. I'm so happy my baby Marquise got us out of Stonebridge."

Her breath caught in her throat.

Her vision blurred, but not enough to miss the first photo.

Marquise. His wife. Their three children.

They all dressed in matching white and gold outfits, standing on the deck of a massive cruise ship, the ocean sparkling behind them like a postcard from paradise. What crushed her heart was that he had a small child.

I didn't know that picture I saw of them in the hospital bed was recent, wow, she thought. How the fuck would I know she groaned.

Marquise wrapped his arm around the woman's waist, his hand resting on the curve of her hip like it belonged there. Like it had never belonged anywhere else. Seeing her hold her newborn with the brightest smile on her face.

His smile—**her** smile—the same one that had coaxed her into believing in forever, was right there on his face. Just as effortless. Just as easy.

She scrolled, her hands trembling.

Photo after photo.

Marquise feeding his wife shrimp cocktail, grinning like a man with a lifetime of love in front of him.

Marquise dancing with his youngest daughter, her hair braided just like her mother's.

Marquise is tossing his son in the air playfully and kissing his infant daughter all over her face. Leilani wanted a child of her own, and it was painful to see the love of her life already have a family.

Marquise and his wife kiss under a sunset sky. **"Twenty Years & Counting"** is in bold letters on the wall behind them.

The room tilted.

A thick, awful weight settled in her chest, squeezing her ribs like a vice.

Her hands felt numb. The phone slid from her fingers, clattering to the floor.

She couldn't breathe.

She had been funding this life.

The plane tickets. The clothes. The extra "business trips."

The damn vacations.

The sickness came fast and brutal. She bolted to the bathroom, barely making it before her stomach heaved. She clutched the toilet, gagging as the betrayal twisted and coiled inside her like something rotten.

When nothing was left, she sagged onto the cold tile, her cheek pressed against it, tears burning tracks down her face.

The silence around her wasn't empty anymore.

It was screaming.

And somewhere deep inside her, **The Girl on the Bus,** the little girl who stayed quiet so nobody would hate her, the one who swallowed her feelings and made herself small so she wouldn't be abandoned, **she** finally started to scream too.

Her phone rang.

She almost ignored it, but when the name flashed across the screen—**Maeve**—she swiped to answer, her breath still shaky.

"You saw it?" Maeve's voice was sharp, no sugar-coating, no hesitation.

Leilani squeezed her eyes shut. "Yeah, I seen that bullshit."

A pause. Then a deep exhale. "Baby girl, you gotta let this man go. You hear me?"

Silence.

"Lani." Maeve's voice softened, but the steel underneath it remained. "He's playing you. He's been playing you. You can't sit there and keep letting him win. He does not deserve you, Leilani. You're better than this shit."

"I know it's hard, and he is all I know. I'm scared to be alone, I don't know if I can do that." Leilani whispered, but it came out hollow, empty.

"No, you **don't** know." Maeve pushed. "If you did, you wouldn't still be in that damn house, breathing in his damn lies. You got me so you will never be alone plus you a bad bitch you will have a new man in no time."

Leilani's throat tightened.

"Pack your shit, **today.** I'm coming to get you."

"Mae—"

"No. No excuses. No second chances. He showed his ass and you can't deny this shit no more. He getting to damn careless so he did this shit to himself. He showed the world who he is and who he loves. Now we gone show his ass how we move the fuck on period.”

Leilani bit her lip, her fingers curling into a fist against the floor.

“You are worth more than this, **you hear me?**” Maeve’s voice cracked. “I love you, but I swear to God, if you let that man crawl back into your life after this, I—” She breathed. “I can’t watch you do this to yourself anymore.”

“I know, Mae, it’s just hard, and I don’t think I know how to move forward.” Leilani cried into the phone. Leilani wiped her face, the weight of it all pressing down on her like an avalanche.

“Say it,” Maeve demanded. “Say you’re leaving. Let me know that you done with this lame ass dude. Leave his ass behind you could be doing so much better.”

Leilani opened her mouth, but the words got stuck.

“Say it.”

Her hands were still shaking. Her heart was still breaking. But she forced the words past her lips.

“I’m leaving.”

And this time, she meant it.

******

It was about two and a half weeks later, and the house was too still. The kind of stillness that pressed down on Leilani's chest, thick and suffocating, like a weighted blanket made of memories she didn't want anymore.

She stood in the middle of the living room, a half-packed box at her feet, eyes sweeping over the space that had been *theirs*—or at least, she had fooled herself into believing it was. Every corner held some trace of him. His sneakers were still kicked under the couch like he was coming back. His blunt ashes were in the tray, as if he had just been there. The hoodie was draped over her favorite chair, which she used to curl up in after work, waiting for him to come home.

A fresh wave of nausea rolled in, but she swallowed it down. She was done throwing up over him.

"Lani."

Mae's voice was soft but steady, cutting through the silence. She stood in the doorway, arms crossed, watching her cousin like she was afraid she might shatter.

Leilani didn't respond, just reached for the hoodie and shoved it into a black trash bag. One more piece of him gone.

Mae sighed and stepped forward, dropping onto the floor beside her. She grabbed Leilani's abandoned box and tossed random junk inside—old receipts, charger cords, whatever wasn't nailed down.

"I'm proud of you, you know that? This is the first step to bettering your life. You will be so much better for it." Mae murmured, taping up the box and pushing it aside.

Leilani exhaled, the sound shaky, her hands still moving, still *doing* because if she stopped, she wasn't sure she'd be able to start again.

"I should've done this long ago," she admitted.

Mae shrugged. "Maybe. But you're doing it now. That's what matters."

Leilani nodded, but the lump in her throat was back, rigid and unmovable.

She pressed her palms against her thighs, forcing her breathing to stay even. No tears. She had none left for him.

Mae reached over, squeezing her wrist. "We don't gotta talk about him. But if you need to talk, like… about what's next, where you're gonna go—"

"I signed a lease, so I'm good, cuz." The words tumbled out before she even realized she was saying them.

Mae's eyebrows lifted. "Wait, what? When? See, that's why you're my favorite cousin. It's nothing for you to bounce back but those emotions might take a while boo."

Leilani laughed a short laugh. "A few days ago, I know you wanted me to come stay with you. But I needed the alone time, and once I found out he would be gone longer than expected, I took advantage of that.

"Damn that's the move cousin I'm glad you were able to find some piece. Shit I would have been in this bitch tearing shit up and throwing out shit. But you're better cuz you're better than me." Mae shook her head.

Leilani laughed at her cousin. "I just needed to know I had a place before moving around. I can't be out here homeless, and I'm not going to my mom's house. You know how I feel about her."

Mae stared at her for a beat, then a slow grin spread across her face. "Look at you. Handling business. I love my cuzzin, you're going to be good. Lei, you're strong; nothing can keep you down. And you know damn well you won't be homeless you could have stayed with me anytime."

Leilani let out a breath and laughed. A laugh she has not felt in a long time.

"Speaking of staying with me, where is his lame ass at? I was expecting him to be in here crying over you leaving." Mae pressed.

"I have not contacted him since you sent their wonderful anniversary celebration for the family. I usually send him encouraging texts, but I have nothing to say. He has texted me a few times, but I have not responded.

Plus, I assume once he came back, he was spending more time in la la land. He lied to me about a work trip, so he has to stay away for some time to make it seem real. Damn I feel so stupid."

Mae nodded like that was enough sadness. "You're not stupid stop saying that you were just with a fake ass man who could hide shit. Man, do it, unfortunately. Sometimes we women want something so bad, and it's hurting us. We can't tell because of the love we have for a man. Anyway, now you got me in my feelings thinking of dumb ass past relationships."

She laughed, changing the subject. Did you need help moving into yo new spot?"

Leilani hesitated. She wanted to say no and insisted that she could do this alone. But the weight in her chest was too much, and for once, she didn't want to carry it alone.

"Girl, yes, of course I would love that. I was planning to go to my new house after this, cuz. I was going to pay for some movers, but I was also waiting for the last minute," she admitted.

Mae nudged her shoulder. "Say less, you know I got you! Plus, I'm trying to see the house. I can't believe you're finally leaving the apartment life. I'm so happy I feel newness coming," she laughed.

"Mae, you play too much. Let's finish this so we can get over to the house. She laughed, engaging in the warmth, overfilling the apartment.

They kept moving, room by room, packing her life away from his—no dramatic speeches. No screaming matches—no texts begging for closure.

Just silence.

The silence she always gave when the pain was too big to speak.

By the time the sun started creeping up, the house was empty—her toothbrush gone from the bathroom, her clothes missing from the closet, even her favorite mug, the one with the chipped handle, safely tucked in her car.

She left a folded note on the kitchen counter with some simple words to Marquise:

I'm done with this shit. I left all your stuff here. You need to get it by the end of the month, or they will throw it out. It's not like you are worried about it, but the lease will be paid in full by the end of the month. So, make sure you get your shit and return their key.

Mae stood by the door, watching her cousin feeling sad and happy for her cousin all at the same time. "You good?"

Leilani inhaled deeply, held it, then let it go.

"Yeah, go ahead, I will lock up."

Mae nodded and walked out the door. She headed to her car, waiting to follow Leilani to her new house.

Leilani looked at the note one last time, then looked over the empty apartment one last time to ensure she was not leaving anything. She turned and walked out the door, locking the apartment up. She then walked over to her U-Haul and hopped in, starting it up.

She drove to the leasing office and dropped the key into the overnight drop box, sealing the end of her journey here. She drove off with Mae following her; it would only take about 22 minutes to get on the other side of Hollis Ridge. She made sure that her new house was not close to this area, but she did not want to move out of Stonebridge completely.

After driving for what felt like forever, she pulled up to a nice neighborhood where her new lovely home sat. She turned down a street named Laxi Ave, and there sat her home, a light blue house with a black roof and a comfortable driveway. Leilani was so proud because she had always seen herself living in an apartment her whole life. This house had two bedrooms, so it was one level, definitely something she could start with.

Excitedly, she hopped out of the U-Haul, looking at Mae getting out of the vehicle.

"Girl, now this is really cute for you. I love this house; it fits you perfectly. Show me the inside first, I need to see what the inside looking like." Mae smiled, getting extra loud and animated, fingers moving and neck popping.

Leilani couldn't do anything but laugh at her leading the way to the front door. She put the key into the lock and opened the door. She walked in, and that fresh new paint smell hit her nose like a joyful moment.

She walked her cousin all through the house—well, Leilani likes to think of it as a flat. She started with the living room and kitchen since they are connected, and what you see first. Then she showed her the cute bathroom with a sexy ass frosty glass door and a shower and bath inside. It should have been illegal how spacious her bathroom was.

Then there were the two bedrooms she saved for last. They headed towards the back of the flat so Leilani could finish mapping it out. Both of the rooms were the same size. However, one had a cute little master bathroom with a bathtub like a Jacuzzi. The other one had a huge closet where you could walk in and sit down if you liked. It had an area where you could put a little couch and chair.

Leilani started talking out loud about her decoration plans. "Shit, I was thinking I could get some fuzzy, cute furniture for this area. Maybe my favorite color, or mixing it up with two powder colors. That shit would be so cute," she said.

"Yes, cousin, I could see that. We could be here while you try those professional blouses and slacks. Then there is me sipping on my drank," she said, dancing.

Leilani laughed, loving how silly her cousin was. She always put her smile on her face. "It's not going to take us too long to get everything in since I don't have a lot of stuff. But I already know this house may change that for me soon," she smiled.

"Yasss cuz I love this house and it's spacious. You could hook this up anyway and keep changing it so it feels new." Mae was so happy for her cousin. She gave her a big, proud hug.

Leilani and Maeve started bringing everything into the living room. After about 30 minutes, Maeve got some chicken and fries so they could stop and eat. After eating, Maeve brought the last of the items from the U-Haul. Leilani was busy putting things in the right place when Maeve felt she had a bright idea.

"Cuz, you keep doing your thing. It's getting late so I am going to get us some tequila we might as well celebrate in this bitch" she yelled dramatically.

"It's not like you're going to let me say no. Just hurry up, bout time you get back, I will be at my stopping point looking for that sip." She looked up at her, showing her seriousness.

Maeve didn't say anything more; she hurried out the door before her cousin changed her mind. She knew the area well; a liquor store was five minutes away.

While Mae was gone, Leilani got to work. She put everything in the bedroom away and moved all the toiletries to their new home. She also made sure to pull out some glasses in case they take shots or mix liquor. She had only had some chairs because she did not take anything from that apartment; a lot of that shit got thrown away. She will figure out that soon enough; there really is no reason to rush; who would she be impressing?

Maeve walked in the door impressed while talking shit. "Girl, bye. I was not gone that long for you to be deep into watching a movie. Like you've been waiting forever," she laughed while setting the bags on the square kitchen island.

"Girl, nobody was worried about you," Leilani laughed. "I got enough done for the day, so I'm good just to chill, pull that liquor out, and leave me alone. She then got up and walked over to the kitchen island.

Mae grabbed the cups Leilani left out for her and filled them with two shots of tequila, some juice, and ice so it would be strong. She gave one to Leilani and put her cup up in the air, signaling a toast.

"To a new beginning, and my cousin leaving a lame, and my cousin getting a new house, and"

"Mae, you're doing the most," Leilani laughed, stopping her crazy speech while raising her cup. Let's just toast to gaining peace and working on loving ourselves," she smiled brightly.

"Hell yeah, cuz I will drink to that".

They both took their drinks, entered the living room, and sat down. Leilani had something playing on the TV, but neither of them was watching. They were too busy talking, reminiscing, and discussing the future while enjoying their drinks. Leilani was happy that she had finally done something for herself and no longer felt guilty about being alone, and Maeve was pleased that her cousin was finally willing to move on and heal.

*

Turning Pain into Purpose

Leilani woke up with a new passion on her mind. She was ready to get to work, not her regular job with a boss who steals her shine. She was prepared to venture out and explore what project management had to offer. Leilani was tired of people dimming her light and downplaying the type of person she is. She wanted to be included in the kind of work that mattered—the kind she had once dreamed about before she lost herself in keeping a man above water while drowning herself.

Project management had always been on her mind. She was good at it without thinking about it, like a silent skill. But now she wanted to put that skill to the test? Now, she was intentional and didn't care about chasing a paycheck; she was pursuing her dreams—this wasn't about anyone but Leilani.

She stayed up late, eyes burning from hours of research, diving into certification requirements, watching YouTube videos on leadership strategies, and taking notes with a hunger she hadn't felt in years.

Every checklist, project plan, and PowerPoint presentation wasn't just busywork. It was rebuilding, reclaiming. Organizing timelines and creating deliverables gave her something she never had before: *control*.

She took a break because she was hungry and had been researching all day. Leilani was glad today was the weekend because there would be no way she could do all this and her job. It felt good putting in work on something that interested her. For so long, she lived her life for others.

If she wasn't handling Marquise's urgent problems, she was wrapped up in doing Mr. Hardling's activities. You know, the activities he wanted nothing to do with.

She got up from the couch and looked at what she could hook up quickly. Looking in the freezer, she jumped happily because she had forgotten about the lasagna she had brought earlier this week. Leilani removed that from the freezer, immediately removed it from the box, and prepared it for the oven. She read that it would take twenty-five minutes.

That's right up my alley. I can put this in and take a shower to get more relaxed before I jump back into this research. She then put her food in the oven, set the timer, and headed to the bathroom.

Once in the bathroom, she turned the shower on and adjusted the temperature to her liking. She wrapped her braids around her hair, as if it were silk-pressed, and then tied them down with a silk scarf. When she was done, she took off her little nightgown, which she had worn to bed, and threw it in the hamper.

Stepping into the shower, she had to let out a little moan; the water was just perfect. She stood there for about 15 minutes, even though it felt like an hour. With her body relaxed, she put on her exfoliated gloves and then hit the top of her body wash four times to get four pumps of soap.

Leilani started at her shoulders and worked her way down to her toes. She made sure to get as much soap as possible on her back by applying a generous amount to the back of her shoulders and letting the water help the soap wash down. She washed up two more times and then hopped out.

She dried her body off and then put on her robe. She walked to her room and grabbed some lotion from her dresser. Taking off her robe, she got every part of her body from top to bottom. Since she was not going anywhere today, she just wore matching blue panties and a bra. She threw on some leggings and a slightly oversized T-shirt.

Walking back to the kitchen, she noticed that her timer was off. "Damn, I bet this shit was already done she said, but that's OK with me." She took her food from the oven and set it on the stove. Her food looked and smelled good. She knew it was done because it was still bubbling when she stuck her face in the pan. She grabbed a plate and cut a nice-sized lasagna. She then covered it with aluminum foil in case she wanted more.

She went and sat on one of the chairs in the living room, moving her computer out of the way, and set her plate down. She turned on a show and enjoyed her quick meal. She wanted another piece, so she grabbed it from the kitchen and continued to watch her show. After finishing, she cleaned her dishes and put away the leftovers. Leilani did not like to leave a mess.

Yes, now I feel good and can get back to my research. I'm so excited, I think something good is going to happen. Leilani smiled to herself.

Later that evening, an email came through from one of the executives at her job—a link to a women's leadership and project management seminar downtown.

"Well, this is interesting. Let me take a look at the agenda."
Once she looked over everything, she felt inspired to
participate in the seminar. She needed this!

She stared at it, the mouse hovering over the
register button.

The old Leilani—the one who stayed small, let
herself shrink, swallowed her voice to keep the peace—
would've ignored it. Would've let doubt creep in,
whispering that she wasn't ready or *good enough*.

But this new Leilani?

The one who had crawled through heartbreak,
wiped her tears, packed her damn bags, and walked out on
a life that was never meant for her?

She clicked **register**.

A weight lifted from her chest.

She had paid more for Marquise and all his
stupid, debt-crippling bullshit. This? This was an investment
in herself.

And the moment she got the confirmation
email, a rush of something close to *pride* filled her chest.
She snatched her phone off the desk, pulling up Mae's
contact.

It barely rang twice before Mae answered. "Tell
me something good, 'Lani."

Leilani exhaled, then grinned. "I just signed up for a project management seminar."

There was a pause. Then—

"SHUT UP. No, you didn't!"

Leilani laughed. "I did. Full weekend seminar. Leadership, networking, career strategy, all of it."

Mae screamed so loud that Leilani had to pull the phone away from her ear. "Girl, finally! Oh my God, you are doing this. You are following your dreams, making moves for Leilani."

"I am, and I can't believe it," Leilani said, softer now, almost to herself.

"You hear that?" Mae said, her voice still buzzing with excitement. "That's the sound of a grown-ass woman *choosing herself*. I'm so damn proud of you, Leilani."

Something in her chest cracked wide open at those words.

She swallowed. "I think... I think I'm proud of myself, too."

Mae sniffed. "Look, you're not about to make me cry on my couch. You *know* I ugly cry."

Leilani smiled, the kind that reached to her bones. "I love you, Mae."

"I love you more, sis."

And for the first time in a long time, Leilani felt she was exactly where she was supposed to be. And it would only get better from here!

**

It was the following weekend, and the conference center lobby was buzzing — women in sleek blazers and bold colors networking like their lives depended on it. Leilani stood by the registration table, clutching her folder, trying not to let the familiar anxiety creep in.

She wasn't used to being **seen.**

As she turned toward the coffee station, she bumped hard into someone, her folder slipping from her hands, papers scattering across the marble floor.

"Damn, my bad," a deep voice said.

She dropped to her knees to grab the papers, and **he dropped down with her.** Tall, dark skin smooth like polished wood, with a beard sharp enough to slice through the bullshit. His fitted dress shirt stretched across broad shoulders, and his eyes — **those eyes — were blunt but curious.**

"You alright?" he asked, handing her one of the many pages scattered across the floor.

"Yeah, I'm good." Her voice was quieter than she wanted it to be.

He didn't move right away. "You here for the seminar?"

She shook her head. "Project management one."

A slow smile tugged at his lips. "Figures. You look like you know how to handle shit."

Heat crept up her neck. "You're not here for the seminar?"

"Nah. Got dragged here by my sister. She said I need to 'network'." He used air quotes, his tone half-amused, half-annoyed.

Leilani's lips twitched into something close to a smile.

"You got a name, project manager?"

"Leilani."

"Leilani." He let it roll off his tongue like he wanted to get the feel of it. Like he was conducting his testing on how it felt in his mouth. "I'm Chemistry and it's nice to meet you."

She blinked. "Like...that's your real name?"

"Nah, but it's what everybody calls me. And trust me —" He stood, offering her his hand, "— the name fits."

She took his hand, the warmth of his palm grounding her for a moment. There was no spark, no cinematic moment of love at first sight — just **solidness.** Like maybe, just maybe, someone saw her.

"Nice to meet you, Chemistry."

"Nice to meet you, too, Leilani."

"Well, I've got to get going. Chemistry, there is so much to learn today. Maybe I will see you later. She said, waving goodbye.

He waved at her as she walked away. *Oh, you don't have to worry about that, Leilani. I'm almost sure I will see you later.* He smiled, walking the other direction. He had to make it seem like he was participating; he did not want to hear his sister Lisa's mouth. He was upset she dragged him here, but maybe it's not such a bad thing now.

Later during one of the sessions, Leilani sat in the back corner of the seminar room, her notebook open in her lap, pen resting against the page, but she wasn't taking notes. Not really.

She was supposed to be focused on the presenter—some polished woman in a tailored blazer talking about "owning your leadership voice." But all Leilani could hear was his voice—that deep, confident tone, the way he said her name like it was **worth saying**.

Chemistry.

She didn't know what it was about him — maybe the easy way he stood, like the world couldn't shake him, or the way his eyes **didn't look through her** but **at her** like she was actually someone worth seeing.

This was new territory in her eyes.

Most men didn't see her unless they needed something. And even then, they only saw the parts that served them — her wallet, body, mind, and silence.

But Chemistry, he didn't want anything. At least, not yet. It seemed too good to be true. And that made her nervous.

Because men like that — men who didn't need her to survive — were dangerous. They made you want to be more, step up, and match their energy. And she wasn't sure if she was ready for things like that. To be pushed like that.

She tapped her pen against the notebook, her knee bouncing under the table. The old her — the one who **shrunk herself down to fit into Marquise's world —** would've written Chemistry off already. Too bold, too comfortable in his skin, too likely to **see through all her cracks**.

But the new her — the one clawing her way out of the wreckage — was curious.

And curiosity could be dangerous, too.

Before she knew it, this session was over, and it was time for the staff to set up for lunch. They had already begun, which took her out of her thoughts.

She chose to leave the room like others, while the staff continued to set up for lunch. Once she was out of the room, she found one of the empty seats in the hall and returned to her thoughts of chemistry.

**

"Why you lookin' so serious?"

His voice slid into her thoughts like warm honey, smooth and slow, a quiet intrusion she almost welcomed. It wasn't until she felt his presence—leaning against her table, arms crossed, that same cocky half-smirk tugging at his lips—that she fully registered him.

Leilani blinked, caught off guard, her fingers tightening around the rim of her coffee cup. "Oh—uh—no reason. Just thinking about some things." She lied knowing damn well she was just thinking of this fine man.

"Thinkin' that hard?" He arched a brow, a knowing glint in his dark eyes. "Might need to take a break before you hurt yourself. I would hate to see you laid out over all that thinking."

She scoffed, but a small, traitorous smile played at her lips. "I'm fine, nothing like would happen over thinking."

"Nah." He tilted his head slightly, gaze never leaving hers. "You sittin' here all in your head, lookin' like you tryna solve the world's biggest mystery. Thought you came here to network." His lips curled around the last word like it was some inside joke.

She let out a short laugh, shaking her head. "I—
"

"C'mon, project manager." He pushed off the table, slipping his hands into his pockets with a lazy confidence that made her pulse skip. "Take a break."

"A break?" She glanced around, as if someone might step in and save her from... what, exactly? The slow pull of his charm? The dangerous way her guard was already slipping?

"Yeah," he also looked around, "it is lunch time, right. You see these people getting to it, setting things up. I saw you over here wondering why you're not going inside to eat." He stepped just a fraction closer, enough that she caught the faint scent of him—clean, woodsy, with a hint of something rich and warm. "So, I figured I would come over and ask if you wanted to take a break and get Lunch. Coffee. Somethin'."

Her first instinct was to say no. To shut this down before he got too close—before she started liking this too much.

But then she heard her voice—Marquise's voice, really—looping in her head.

You always act like you're too good for anything. You never take chances. Nobody is checking for you anyway. It wouldn't matter if you went, you think he will call you back.

She swallowed hard.

"I..." Her hesitation lingered, but his expression stayed patient, his smirk softening just enough to feel like an invitation instead of a dare.

"It's just lunch," he said, voice low, smooth as a promise. "I ain't proposing."

That made her laugh, the sound spilling out before she could stop it.

"Yes, let's do it," she said, surprising herself. "Lunch."

A full grin broke across his face then—sharp, confident, devastatingly sexy. The kind of grin that made her stomach dip made her wonder what else he could talk her into.

"Cool." He nodded toward the door. "Let's go before you change your mind."

And just like that, Leilani let herself take a chance.

*

Breaking Down Walls

The small café was buzzing — not too loud, but enough background noise to ensure they weren't overheard. Leilani stirred her iced tea with the thin black straw, watching the ice swirl and melt, as if the answer to why she was sitting here with this man might be floating somewhere in her cup.

What am I even doing here?

It was supposed to be a quick lunch—polite conversation, maybe some professional chit-chat about career paths and industry trends, nothing more.

But from the second Chemistry slid into the seat across from her, his presence filled the space, making it impossible to retreat into herself like she usually did.

"You're always this quiet, or is it just me?" His voice was playful, but there was something in his eyes — a sharpness as he saw straight through the surface.

Leilani's lips curved into a small, almost shy smile. "I'm not quiet. I'm just... observing."

"Oh, you're one of those types." He leaned back in his chair, his broad shoulders stretching his shirt just enough to catch her attention. "Quiet ones always got the most to say — you just waitin' to see if I'm worth talkin' to."

She laughed, surprising herself with how natural it felt. "Maybe."

"Fair enough." He took a sip of his water, his eyes never leaving her. "So, what made you come to this seminar? You tryna switch up careers, or you just here for the free snacks?"

That made her laugh again, and this time it reached her eyes. "Nah, I'm serious about project management. It's something I've wanted for a long time."

"Why?" His tone was easy, but the question was unexpectedly direct — not just small talk, but curiosity with weight behind it.

Her fingers tightened around her glass. **Why?**

Because I want to be in control for once.

Because I'm tired of being the one everyone uses.

Because I want to know what it feels like to lead instead of follow.

Because I want to matter.

But she couldn't say all that. Not yet.

"It's just... I like putting things together. Making sense out of chaos." She smiled, but it was thinner now, not quite reaching her eyes.

Chemistry's gaze stayed on her, too sharp for comfort. "Mmm. Sounds like you're talking about more than projects."

Her stomach fluttered — part nerves, part thrill — at how quickly he caught the undercurrent of her words. She felt exposed, like her skin was too thin around him.

She tried to retreat into herself, to fold up her feelings into neat little boxes where no one could touch them. But Chemistry didn't leave her the space.

"Relax," he said, his voice low and warm like it was meant just for her. "Ain't nobody askin' for all your secrets today."

That should've made her feel better, but somehow, it made her feel even more vulnerable — because, for once, someone knew there were secrets.

"So, what about you?" she asked, desperate to shift the spotlight off herself. "What do you do?"

He grinned. "You really wanna know, or you just tryna flip the script?"

"Maybe both."

He chuckled, the sound deep and rich. "Fair enough. I do some consulting work, such as business development and management training. Help people get their shit together."

Leilani arched an eyebrow, amusement flickering in her gaze. "You must be good at it," she said, a teasing edge creeping into her voice. "You sound like you got it all figured out."

"Hell nah." His grin widened effortlessly, with a self-assured expression. "But I know how to spot when somebody else's shit ain't together either."

She smirked. "And what exactly does that mean?"

He leaned back slightly, stretching one arm over the back of the chair like he had all the time in the world. "It means I teach people how to move smarter. How to manage risk. How to understand their market and play the game right."

"That sounds like a business class."

"It is," he said smoothly. "Just not the kind they teach in school."

His voice was almost hypnotic—like he was peeling back layers, making her see something differently without realizing it.

"I break things down for people," he continued. "Most folks out here hustling? They think short-term. Fast money, quick flips, no strategy. That's why they don't last. They don't know how to reinvest, keep their overhead low, or move without drawing attention."

She tilted her head, studying him. "And you do?"

He met her gaze without hesitation. "I do."

The weight in his voice, the certainty—it was almost unsettling. He wasn't just talking; he believed every word.

"And you teach other people?"

"I build teams," he corrected. "Structure. Discipline. You don't just run up money—you run a system. You put the right people in place, make sure everybody eats, so nobody gets desperate. Keep everything tight, clean."

The way he described it was strangely corporate, like he was talking about a startup instead of something illegal. It was unsettling and impressive at the same time.

Leilani tapped her fingers against the table, watching him. "So, you're the CEO?"

He chuckled again, slow and knowing. "You could say that."

She didn't know whether to be impressed or concerned. Maybe both.

Leilani felt her breath catch for a second. Was it that obvious? Was her damage hanging off her like a worn-out coat? But before the panic could settle in her chest, Chemistry leaned forward, resting his elbows on the table.

"Look," he said, softer this time, but steel was beneath it. "I know you got your guard up. I get it. But you came to lunch with me — so that means somethin'. Even if you don't know what yet."

Her heart beat unevenly in her chest. It wasn't even what he said — it was how he said it, like he wasn't asking her for anything and naming what was already there between them.

"Why are you so confident?" she asked, half-teasing, half-genuinely curious. "You act like you know me."

"I don't." His eyes locked onto hers, dark and steady. "But I know strength when I see it."

That caught her off guard.

"I know what it looks like when somebody's had to hold themselves together for so long, they don't even realize how heavy it is anymore," he said. "When they don't expect anybody to notice, let alone carry some of that weight."

Her fingers tightened around her glass. "You reading me like a book, huh?"

He smirked, but there was no playfulness in his gaze. "Nah, I just pay attention."

Her stomach flipped, not just at his words, but at how he said them—like there was no doubt in his mind that he was right about her.

"What else do you see?" she asked, before she could stop herself.

His smirk deepened, like he'd been waiting for that question. "I see somebody who's got shit to prove. To herself. To everybody. But mostly to herself."

Leilani swallowed. He wasn't wrong.

"Somebody who's careful," he continued. "Too careful. Who doesn't take chances 'cause she's scared she might not know what to do if things don't go as planned."

She let out a short, breathless laugh, shaking her head. "You just got all the answers, huh?"

"Nah," he said, sitting back, his confidence effortless. "But I got good instincts."

She studied him but was unsure what to do with any of this. It wasn't just what he said; it was how she wanted to believe him.

"Don't overthink this, Leilani," he added, his voice dropping to something low and knowing. "It's just lunch."

Just lunch.

But it already felt like something more.

Was this a date? Or was she reading too much into it? The thought had been nagging at her since the moment Chemistry sat across from her, all easy confidence and sharp observations. She hadn't planned for this to be more than a casual lunch or a simple conversation. But the way he spoke to her and saw her made it feel like something else entirely.

And that was the part that unsettled her the most. How could someone she had just met make her feel more understood in a single conversation than the man she had been with for years?

Chemistry didn't just ask questions to be polite; he didn't nod along distractedly like he was waiting for his turn to speak. No, he listened. He cared more about her thoughts and ideas than any man ever had. It was disarming. A little terrifying. And, if she was being honest, exhilarating.

Man, could this date get any better?

Wait.

Date?

She nearly choked on her drink. Had she just thought that? Was that what this was? Her fingers curled around her glass as she stared at Chemistry, who was watching her with that same unreadable expression. Maybe it wasn't a date. Perhaps it was just lunch. But if that was true, then why did it already feel like more than that?

The little bistro was tucked away in a quiet corner. It felt like a secret, something you only found if you were meant to. The sun spilled through the windows, dappling the wooden table where Leilani and Chemistry sat, plates half-cleared and conversation flowing easily between them.

Leilani's guard had come down just a little. Maybe it was how Chemistry's smile softened when she talked about her childhood dream of running things — how she organized her stuffed animals like they were employees, handing out "assignments" and giving them pretend performance reviews. Or maybe it was just how he listened — not just nodding but hearing her.

"And your first big project was a teddy bear union strike?" Chemistry teased, his deep chuckle rolling through the space between them, warm and rich.

Leilani grinned, stabbing a piece of her salad with her fork. "Hey, they had demands." She pointed at him with her fork, as if making a serious case. "Fair wages, snack breaks, and scheduled nap times. They weren't playing around."

Chemistry leaned back, nodding like he was genuinely considering it. "Damn. Sounds like you ran a tight operation."

"You know it. I had charts, negotiation tactics, the whole deal." She smirked. "Even wrote up a contract. Glitter gel pens and all."

"I can see it now—lil' boss Leilani, clipboard in hand, not takin' no shit."

She laughed, but the sound wavered briefly, her fingers tightening around her fork. "Something like that," she murmured.

Because, yeah, that little girl had thought she could change things. Had believed that if she planned well enough, organized tightly enough, and made herself indispensable enough, the world would have to listen. But she quickly learned that the world didn't care about her lists or plans. It cared about silence. About shrinking.

And that was precisely what she wasn't doing today.

Chemistry watched her, that teasing grin fading just a little, something sharper settling behind his eyes. "You still got that in you," he said, voice quieter now. More serious.

Leilani blinked. "Got what in me?"

"That boss. The one who don't take no shit. The one who organizes, negotiates, sees the bigger picture before anybody else even knows what they're looking at." He tilted his head, studying her like he was seeing something she hadn't even recognized in herself. "You know how rare that is?"

She let out a short laugh, shaking her head. "Come on, Chemistry. It's not that deep. It was just some stuffed animals."

"Nah." His gaze locked on hers, unwavering. "It ain't just that. You've got a mind for project management. Structure, strategy, execution—that's what you do. You've just been doing it without realizing it. And my job? My job is finding talent and expanding it."

Something in her chest tightened, something she wasn't ready to name. Because nobody had ever told her that before. Nobody had looked at the way her brain worked and seen potential instead of a nuisance.

She picked up her glass, taking a slow sip. "So, what, you're some kinda talent scout now?"

He smirked. "Somethin' like that." Then he leaned forward, resting his arms on the table. "Have you ever thought about what you could do if you leaned into that skill? If you stopped tryin' to fit into other people's plans and started building your own?"

Leilani stared at him, heart thudding unevenly. She hadn't. Not really. But damn if the idea didn't make her want to.

What she didn't know—what she couldn't see—was the pair of eyes locked on her from across the restaurant.

***

Marquise.

He was supposed to be having a nice lunch with his wife—their little midday "date," the kind of thing they did to keep up appearances. His wife sat across from him, scrolling through the menu like she wasn't already gonna order the same Caesar salad she always did, snapping a quick pic of the menu for her Instagram story.

"We should do a Q&A on TikTok about our anniversary trip," she said, still glued to her phone. "That would trend since they are still on our anniversary trip. I already got like two thousand likes on the balcony video. You know, the one where I had the mimosa and the little robe on? I should've brought my ring light, though. The lighting was so bad."

Marquise barely nodded, half-focused on stirring the ice in his water.

His wife, unfazed, kept talking. "I think I should start doing GRWM videos—like 'Get Ready With Me: Wife Edition' or something. Oh! And then, I could do a 'Day in the Life of a Bad Bitch Wife.' Like, gym, nail appointment, then pickin' up the kids—" She caught sight of herself in the reflection of her phone and adjusted her hair. "Damn, I should've done my edges this morning."

Marquise still wasn't listening.

Because there was Leilani, sitting at a sunlit table across the restaurant with some dude, laughing like he had never seen her laugh before. Free. Unbothered. Glowing in a way that made his stomach twist.

That's my woman.

His wife was still talking, flipping through her camera roll, admiring her selfies. "We should do another vacation soon. Maybe somewhere bougie. Like the Maldives. Or Dubai. You know how many influencers brand deals I could get out there?"

She was glued to it, watching her latest post blow up in real-time — selfies of her and Marquise, captioned "20 years strong and still growing #BlackLove #AnniversaryVibes #PowerCouple." The likes were rolling in by the second, the comments full of heart emojis and "goals" and people talking about how beautiful their family was.

She finally looked up at him, eyes narrowing. "Are you even listening?"

"Yeah," he muttered, dragging his gaze away from Leilani, even though he already knew—he'd rather sit across from her.

It didn't matter that his wife was across the table, speaking to him, trying to pull him back into the moment. It didn't matter that Leilani had ghosted him like it was nothing—moved out, disappeared, only leaving me a damn note. All that mattered was that she was here now. In this room. Laughing like she wasn't the blueprint. She hadn't once traced every part of him and called it hers.

And now?

Now she was sitting there smiling at another man like Marquise hadn't built her from heartbreak and ambition, from midnight talks and shared struggle, like he hadn't bled for her.

He kept his cool on the outside. But his hand gripped his water glass so tightly that the condensation slid unnoticed. His knuckles turned white, and his jaw clenched so hard it ached.

Leilani leaned in toward the strange man—who the fuck was he anyway? —and laughed at something he said. Her eyes sparkled in that way that used to belong to Marquise—used to.

His wife tried to follow his line of sight, then looked back at him. "Do you know her or something?"

He didn't answer. Couldn't. Because Leilani had just tucked a loose curl behind her ear—his favorite move, the one that meant she was listening—and then touched the strange man's wrist as she excused herself to the bathroom.

Marquise tracked every step she took, the sway of her hips, the confidence in her walk that hadn't dimmed since she left. That hadn't belonged to him in a long time.

The strange man leaned back in his chair, satisfied and smug, watching Leilani's retreat like he'd already won.

Marquise saw red.

He was on his feet before his wife could finish her sentence, voice trailing off in confusion. He didn't care. He wasn't thinking. Not really.

All he knew was Leilani had left the table—and he wasn't about to waste his second chance.

Leilani had just washed her hands, her fingers still damp, as she reached for a paper towel when she felt it—that shift in the air, that presence.

That scent.

Expensive cologne, just a little too heavy, the kind that always lingered long after he left. It had clung to her pillows. Her clothes. Her skin. Back when she didn't know better.

Her stomach dropped before she even turned around.

"Leilani," Marquise's voice came low, almost soft. But she knew that softness. It wasn't affection—it was the hush before the blow. The quiet before he unleashed whatever storm he dragged around in his chest. "You gon act like this?"

She froze only for a second, then forced herself to look up. Met his eyes in the mirror. His reflection stood behind her like a ghost—one she had finally laid to rest, and yet here he was again, trying to claw his way back into the life she'd reclaimed.

"What are you doing here?" she asked, her voice cold, detached. Practiced.

"I should be askin' you that," he said, stepping closer like he had every right. "You disappear like a thief in the night, no word, no explanation—and now you're sitting up here having lunch with some clown?"

Clown.

Her jaw ticked. The way he said it—so casual, so arrogant, like he still had a claim to her.

"Don't do this, Marquise."

"Do what?" he challenged. "Ask my woman why she's moving funny? That's what we do now? After everything I've been through with you? You just bounce and go eat salads with random niggas like I'm nobody?"

She turned around and then slowly pressed her back against the sink. Her Heart was pounding, but her face didn't give it away.

"I'm not your woman."

"The hell you not?" he growled. "You mine, Leilani. Always been mine."

She swallowed, eyes locked on his. "You're here with your wife, Marquise. Your *wife*. You've got a whole life with her. Go back to it."

His lip curled. "You've always been dramatic. You knew what this was. You knew about her, and you still stayed. You *wanted* to stay. You wanted to help me win. You always said, ' I wanna see you shine, baby.' What happened to that?"

"What happened," she said through clenched teeth, "is that I woke up."

He stepped closer, almost chest to chest now. His voice dropped even lower, the words more venom than sound.

"You've always been too sensitive. That's why you never gon make it without me."

That part still stung. He knew exactly where to hit. Knew the right angles to twist.

But this time, it didn't land how he thought it would.

Because this time, Leilani was different. Stronger. Wiser. Tired—but not broken.

She straightened her spine like steel. Calm washed over her like armor. Her voice was slow but steady.

"I already made it," she said. "And you can't stand it."

His jaw clenched. Fists at his sides. No clever comeback. No manipulation left to pull. Just silence and a man realizing he'd lost control—for good.

Leilani didn't wait for him to say anything. She stepped around him, graceful, like he was an obstacle. Her heels clicked against the tile as she walked out, never looking back.

When she got back to the table, Chemistry looked up. His eyes scanned her face, not possessive, not entitled. Just present. Concerned.

"Leilani, you good?" he asked.

She sat, smoothed her napkin across her lap, and nodded. "Yeah," she said, soft but sure. "I'm good."

She was angry on the inside, but she didn't want to reveal it yet. Her chest still ached, and her hands were still trembling from anger. How dare this motherfucker talk to me and he is here with his wife.

But for the first time, she knew – she would be.
**

Leilani slid back into her seat, the ghost of Marquise's presence still clinging to her skin like cigarette smoke—stale, suffocating, inescapable. She lifted her water glass, hoping the cold would steady her trembling hands, forcing her face into the calm, familiar mask she'd worn most of her life.

But Chemistry saw straight through it.

His eyes softened, concern flickering deep beneath the surface, as he leaned forward and lowered his voice. "What's wrong, Leilani?"

"Nothing," she lied automatically, dropping her gaze to her barely-touched salad, feeling like the awkward girl she used to be—the quiet girl on the bus, headphones in, praying nobody noticed her. The one desperate to please everyone, even if it meant breaking herself in the process.

"Don't do that," Chemistry said gently but firmly, resting his elbows on the table and leaning closer, closing the distance she had placed between herself and the world. "I see you, Leilani. What's going on?"

She exhaled shakily, the mask slipping away inch by painful inch. "It's someone I used to know."

"The same someone who had you looking like you're drowning just now?" His voice remained calm and patient, leaving no doubt that he genuinely cared.

Leilani's eyes flickered up, startled by how easily he'd read her. "You saw that?"

"Yeah," Chemistry nodded, unwavering. "Who is he?"

She bit down on her lip, considering holding back—but Chemistry's gaze was open, honest, waiting for her truth without judgment. It made hiding pointless. "Marquise. My ex."

"The same one sitting across from his wife, like he didn't just corner you?" Chemistry's tone darkened slightly, protective energy radiating from him.

Shame surged hot through her chest. "You saw that too, huh?"

"I see more than you think," Chemistry said, his voice steady, grounding her. "Let me guess—you spent years carrying him, building him up, thinking your sacrifices meant something, even while he chose someone else?"

Her eyes stung with unshed tears, her chest aching under the weight of the truth he spoke so effortlessly. "Yeah," she whispered. "Something like that, and yes, I was a fool."

"No," Chemistry corrected immediately, his voice a gentle reassurance she hadn't known she needed. "You were loyal. You were out here taking out loans fucking up your credit with late fees while he was living it up debt free. Trust me, Leilani, I have seen this time and time again. These lames know how to waste good women's time. That doesn't make you foolish—it makes you stronger than most."

His words broke something loose inside her, tears blurring her vision. "I just wanted to be enough."

Chemistry reached across the table, gently placing his hand near hers, not touching, just offering support, patience, and choice. "You were always enough. You just gave it to someone who couldn't appreciate it. That's on him, Leilani—not you."

Her heart pounded; every insecurity she'd buried surfaced in the safety of his presence. "I thought if I stayed quiet and went along, it wouldn't hurt as much. I thought I was protecting myself, but really, I was disappearing."

"You're done hiding," Chemistry said firmly, leaning close enough to anchor her gaze to his. "You deserve to be seen, Leilani. To be loved without conditions. Without fear. You deserve someone who helps you grow, not shrinks you."

The sincerity in his eyes held her steady, and for the first time, hope sparked deep inside her chest. She wasn't sure if she could fully trust it yet, trust him, but she knew one thing clearly:

Chemistry wasn't here to take from her. He was here to help her rise, not for himself, but because he genuinely wanted to see her shine.

"Are you ready to stop carrying ghosts, Leilani?" he asked gently, inviting her to reclaim herself. "Because when you are, I'm right here."

And even though the answer was too tangled inside her to unravel at that moment, for the first time fully, Leilani believed she wouldn't have to do it alone.

Leilani swirled her straw in her water, the ice clinking softly, her mind tangled in all the things she wanted to say — and all the things she was afraid to say out loud.

Chemistry was watching her again, but not like other men usually did. His eyes didn't burn with shallow hunger, didn't roam her body to claim her as his. Instead, his gaze traced her softly, intimately, like he memorized her every breath and subtle shift, preparing himself just in case she slipped through his fingers.

"What are you thinking right now?" His voice was low, warm enough to slip beneath her skin.

Leilani froze, fingers tightening her grip on her glass. "What?"

He tilted his head slightly, eyes locked onto hers with deliberate intensity. "You're over there spinning that straw like it's gonna give you answers." A soft smile teased his lips, but there was an unmistakable weight in his gaze. "So, tell me—what's goin' on up there?"

Her pulse quickened. She felt transparent, exposed in a way she hadn't experienced in years—maybe ever. Everything in her wanted to retreat, to deflect with humor or a casual dismissal, but something in Chemistry's steady presence made those defenses feel useless, flimsy.

Finally, softly, she admitted, "I'm telling myself not to trust this. Not to trust you."

Chemistry didn't flinch, didn't pull back. Instead, he leaned subtly closer, closing the gap between them, his voice quiet but firm. "That's fair. You don't know me."

She swallowed hard, meeting his gaze despite the heat blooming under her skin. "I don't," she whispered. "But somehow...I feel like I do."

His eyes darkened, intensity swirling there—something protective, possessive yet gentle. It felt like safety and danger all at once. "That's because I see you, Leilani."

The way he said her name, slow and intentional, sent a shiver down her spine, lighting a fire deep within her chest. It wasn't possessive—deeper, more profound, like he'd spoken her into existence. Like he'd known her name long before she walked into this moment.

"That's the problem," she murmured, feeling her walls crumbling faster than she could rebuild them.

Chemistry leaned back comfortably, his posture relaxed, but the energy radiating from him felt electric and undeniable. His arms stretched wide along the booth, quietly signaling strength and shelter—a haven he offered without words.

"Nah," he said, his voice like velvet, wrapping around her with warmth and promise. "The real problem is, you've been taken advantage of so long, you forgot what it feels like when somebody sees you. When somebody truly wants you, beyond what you can do for them."

His words stroked every hidden insecurity, every secret longing she'd buried deep beneath self-doubt and silent sacrifices. She felt herself soften, breathing easier, losing herself in the quiet power of his gaze.

"Do you always talk like this?" she finally asked, voice trembling slightly, her heart drumming against her ribs.

"Only when it matters," Chemistry replied, a slow, sexy smile curling the corner of his lips—dangerous and inviting.

The air shifted between them again, becoming heavier and charged with unspoken promise. Leilani felt warmth spread through her body, loosening knots she'd held for far too long, and a sense of quiet longing pooled in her stomach.

"Lunch was supposed to be casual," she breathed, half-laughing, half-nervous, desperate to ease the ache of anticipation settling deep within her.

Chemistry's smile deepened, eyes glittering softly with restrained heat. "Casual's boring. And you deserve more than that."

She didn't say a word, couldn't trust herself to speak—but the silent look she shared with him spoke volumes, echoing the quiet truth they'd both felt at first glance.

She shook her head, but her smile betrayed her. "You're always this direct?"

"Only when I see something I want."

Her heart stuttered, heat flooding her cheeks. She didn't know if he meant the food, the conversation, or her.

But she wanted to find out.

*

Breaking Down Barriers

Across the room, Marquise sat stiffly in his seat, his food untouched and cooling rapidly. His eyes were fixed somewhere else entirely—somewhere far from his wife's constant chatter.

His wife, however, seemed oblivious. Her voice was a nonstop stream of excitement, her eyes locked on the glowing screen of her phone.

"Baby, look! This one got over 500 likes already!" she practically squealed, thrusting her phone toward his face. When he barely glanced at it, irritation flickered behind her smile. "People are saying we're couple goals. Do you see this?"

Marquise grunted noncommittally; gaze distant. His indifference made her blood boil.

Inside, she rolled her eyes. If only these people knew the truth—their perfect "couple goals" image was a manufactured illusion. She cared less about family, commitment, or love. Her priority was the followers, likes, shares, and comments. The rush of validation kept her going.

"Are you even listening to me?" she snapped, voice sharp as she set the phone down with a loud clatter against the table. Her carefully constructed smile vanished, replaced by annoyance. "I'm trying to celebrate our success, and you're acting like you're somewhere else."

Marquise exhaled sharply, pulling himself back from

whatever far-off place he'd disappeared to. "You're celebrating likes, not success," he said flatly.

She narrowed her eyes, leaning in slightly to keep their argument private but intense. "Those likes keep the lights on. Those likes to pay the bills. Do you think people care if we're happy? They care that we look happy. So, act like it."

He shook his head slowly, his jaw tight, resentment etched deep into his features. "Maybe I'm tired of acting."

Her expression hardened further, eyes sparking with barely concealed anger. "Too bad. This is what we built. This pays for your expensive tastes, clothes, cologne, and everything else. If you mess this up, it's on you."

She lifted her phone again, forcing a smile back onto her face as she flipped the camera towards them. "Now smile," she ordered quietly, urgently. "We have followers watching."

Marquise reluctantly shifted closer, forcing his features into a hollow imitation of happiness as the camera flashed—a perfect illusion masking a truth neither dared to face.

Marquise forced a smile, nodding like he gave a damn. But his mind was somewhere else. He found himself reminiscing about a memory with Leilani.

A smell had triggered it. A faint trace of smoked bread drifted from the kitchen, and just like that, a memory returned.

**

Marquise used his key to enter the apartment and saw Leilani, whose face lit up with a big smile.

"I made dinner," she'd said, smiling, her voice soft, full of hope. "You didn't eat, right?"

She was so excited and had rushed home from work. She had the slow jams going in the background. She cooked his favorite meal: carrots, smothered mashed potatoes, and lamb chops. When she heard him coming in, she removed her scarf while quickly taking the cornbread out of the oven.

He didn't look at her. Just muttered, "Nah, I'm good." He said, walking over to the couch and sitting down.

Her heart had dipped, but she stayed steady. "You sure? It's your favorite."

"I said I'm good, Leilani." Marquise picked up the remote and started flipping through the channels. "I heard about this funny ass show. Come watch this shit with me," he said while twisting up a blunt and opening a bottle of Hennessey.

It wasn't just the words. It was the weight behind them. Like her care was a burden.

She sat beside him anyway, hoping proximity could fill the silence. When she reached for his hand, trying to hold a piece of him, he snatched it back like her touch burned.

"What show do you want to watch?" she asked. "Please don't tell me it's that reality TV mess." Leilani hated

watching those types of shows. The cast seemed degrading to their race, and they would stop at nothing to become famous.

His eyes stayed glued to the screen. "What's wrong with reality shows. Bring some entertainment around here. Sometimes it be drier than a motherfucker over here."

"Damn this post has 30,000 likes look as this Marquise."

His wife's excitement pulled him from a memory involving Leilani. He was upset because this was the first time he noticed Leilani's love for him. He was annoyed by his wife going on about that damn social media.

His wife was everything the world told him was perfect — outgoing, social, and a catch. But sitting across from her now, with her eyes glued to her screen and her mouth running a mile a minute, all he felt was empty.

Leilani had been his calm. His quiet place. The one person who didn't need him to be anyone but himself — and the only one who saw him, even when he was at his worst.

Her quietness, her softness, her way of making herself small — it used to frustrate him, but now? Now, it was all he could think about.

She never needed a spotlight. Never needed likes, comments, or anything viral to feel whole. She wasn't performing for anyone. She was just... there. For him. In the shadows, making sure he was good, even when she wasn't.

And now, she was gone. Sitting across from another man, laughing, that soft laugh that used to be his.

That shit burned.

He clenched his fork, his mind racing. He wasn't about to let her go. Not for good. Leilani was his peace, safe space, and escape from all this noise.

He'd do whatever it took to get her back.

Whatever it took.

*

Back at the table, Leilani's hand stilled, her breath deeper now. She met Chemistry's gaze—steady, warm, and waiting.

She smiled. This time, it reached her eyes.

Because for so long, she'd told herself she was too much. Too soft. Too needy.

But the truth was, she had loved hard, and he hadn't known what to do with that kind of gold.

"I used to think it was my fault," she said quietly, almost more to herself than to Chemistry. "Like I asked for too much. But really... I just wanted what I gave."

Chemistry didn't say anything. He just looked at her like she made sense. Like her words were worth space.

Leilani leaned back in her seat, shoulders relaxed.

She wasn't ashamed anymore.

She didn't regret loving him. She just felt grateful she had survived it.

And now?

She was still here. Still whole. And finally, learning how to love herself the way she once loved him.

The waitress slid the check onto the table, but neither reached for it immediately. Their conversation had slowed to a comfortable lull, where silence didn't feel awkward — just full of things neither of them was ready to say out loud.

Leilani glanced down at her hands, her fingers tracing the edge of her water glass. "Thanks for lunch," she said softly. "I wasn't expecting... all of this."

"All of what?" Chemistry asked, leaning in just a little, that steady gaze still locked on her.

She exhaled, shaking her head. "I don't know. You. The way you talk to me like you know me."

For a moment, she was nervous. Did she want to let him in, only to be left again? This brought back a flashback from when Leilani was eight years old.

****

Leilani had two siblings, and it was a bright sunny day. Her sister was seven, and her brother was six years old. They were playing outside when Leilani heard her mother calling her from downstairs. She was upstairs, devising a master plan.

Leilani ran down the stairs. "Yes, Mom."

"Why are you not outside with your brother and sister? This is why you are always left behind. You are never with most of the kids."

"I'm sorry, Mom, I was just sitting there thinking about some things," Leilani said with innocent eyes.

"Leilani, we talked about this. What are you even thinking about at eight years old? You must focus on learning to interact with other children your age. This child's development is significant, and you're wasting your time thinking about lord knows what."

"I am going outside now," she said, walking towards the door. I was only thinking about organizing a project that my brother, sister, and I could do together. We need to earn some money so we can buy more candy.

"Make sure, Leilani, your siblings are in this house before the street lights come on. Don't make me have to come find y'all asses, " her mother yelled. She continued off the porch towards her siblings; she would finish her brainstorming later.

"Maybe I do," he said, snapping her from her memory, that slight smirk tugging at the corner of his mouth again. "Maybe I know a woman who's been holding her breath for too damn long."

She felt that — deep. "It's been a long time since

someone saw me like that," she said, almost a whisper. "I forgot what it felt like."

Before she could respond, he slid his card onto the bill and handed it to the waitress, maintaining eye contact. "Lunch is on me," he said, leaving no room for argument.

Leilani didn't fight it. For once, it felt good to let someone else take care of something, even if it was just a meal.

As they stood to leave, Chemistry's hand hovered at the small of her back — not touching, just close enough to remind her he was there.

"You alright?" he asked as they stepped onto the sidewalk.

She nodded, even though her chest felt tight with the weight of all the feelings she hadn't sorted through. "I will be."

He held her gaze for a long beat before nodding. "Good. Since I'm not done getting to know you." He smiled at her.

The way he said it wasn't a question — it was a promise. And Leilani felt like someone meant it for the first time in a long time.

**

Opportunity Knocking

Leilani had been in the office since before sunrise. She was the first to unlock the glass doors, the first to refill the stale coffee in the break-room, and the last to leave most nights, though her name was never the one mentioned in the recap emails.

Today was no different. Her boss, Mr. Harding, had dumped three project decks on her desk with a casual, "Need these cleaned up before ten o'clock," before disappearing into his office with a fresh cup of coffee and his ego.

She didn't flinch. She just got to work. Slide by slide, chart by chart, she wove the story together—the strategy, the market data, the insights. Her fingerprints were all over the presentation, even if no one would ever know.

By the time the meeting started, she'd been running on fumes and willpower, but her expression stayed composed. Neutral. Professional.

Mr. Harding stood at the head of the sleek conference table, smiling like he'd built the deck himself. "Let's dive in, shall we?" he said, clicking the remote like he was conducting a symphony.

Mr. Taylor, one of the senior VPs, sat across the table, silent but observant. He watched Harding closely, but his eyes often flicked to Leilani, especially when Harding stumbled through explanations she had typed word for word.

When the presentation wrapped and applause echoed around the room, Harding chuckled and said, "Guess those late nights are finally paying off." The room laughed with him.

Leilani's jaw clenched. She kept her smile tight, eyes lowered as the department heads nodded and congratulated Mr. Hardling on a job well done.

She never said a word.

But Mr. Taylor was watching.

He noticed she didn't flinch when her work credit was stolen. The way she carried herself, head high, even when overlooked. There was strength there. Quiet, understated, but undeniable.

At the post-presentation recap, Mr. Taylor moved closer as coffee cups were being refilled, and everyone buzzed with anticipation for the next steps.

"You did excellent work," he said quietly, just loud enough for her to hear.

She blinked, startled, looking up at him.

He didn't smile. Just gave a nod, respectful. "I saw you, Leilani."

Leilani felt something shift in her chest. Not gratitude. Not pride.

Recognition.

And for the first time in a long time, she let herself feel it.

**

Later that afternoon, as she gathered her things to leave, Mr. Taylor appeared beside her desk. Not looming, just present.

"Ms. Brooks," he said smoothly, folding his arms. "Mind walking with me for a second?"

She nodded cautiously, stepping beside him as they moved toward the elevator.

They stood in silence for a beat before he spoke again.

"I hear you're attending the project management seminar downtown."

Her brows lifted in surprise. "How did you—? I didn't tell anyone."

He gave her a knowing glance. "You didn't have to. Word gets around when people pay attention."

She looked away, slightly embarrassed, unsure if she was about to be reprimanded for stepping outside her lane.

Mr. Taylor continued, "I wanted to give you a heads-up—someone will be approaching you there. Don't be surprised when they offer you a wonderful opportunity. ... keep your ears open."

Leilani blinked. "An opportunity? What kind of—"

He gave her a half-smile, then checked his watch. "Let's just say, good work doesn't go unnoticed forever."

Before she could ask more, he nodded once, stepping back. "Enjoy the seminar."

She stood there in the hallway, heart racing, mind spinning.

She hadn't even wanted anyone to know she was trying to grow beyond her current role. She'd signed up for that seminar late at night, on a whisper of a dream she was afraid to speak aloud.

But Mr. Taylor knew.

And maybe—maybe—her hard work was finally starting to speak for itself.

The next day, she attended the seminar's final day. The seminar was nearly over, and she had yet to meet someone. Doubt was creeping in, and she thought maybe the VP was pulling her arm. How would he know the work she did anyway? Mr. Harding has all the credit and notoriety, she thought.

Leilani felt a light touch on her arm, snapping her from negative thoughts. She turned to see a polished but approachable woman with a warm smile and sharp eyes.

"I've been watching you during the workshops, and I also know Mr. Taylor," the woman said. "How you think through problems and work with others — you've got something special. I have heard nothing but great things about your work. I have been told you are very organized and have heightened attention to detail."

Leilani blinked, caught off guard. "Oh… wow. Thank you. Wait, Mr. Taylor told you things about me, I can't believe it."

The woman extended her hand. "I'm Simone Carter. I run a project management firm here in the city. Yes, Mr. Taylor has had his eyes on you for a few years now. He believes you have true potential and are not fully utilized at your current job. We're always looking for interns who show real potential, and I think you'd be a great fit."

Leilani's heart skipped. "You want me to come and work for you?"

"Absolutely," Angela said firmly. "You have a natural leadership presence, even when you don't realize it. I'd love to help you get into project management and see how you grow. I have already talked to Mr. Taylor about this, and he is willing to provide you with a severance package."

"Wait, what do you mean by a severance package? They are willing to pay me to get another job. What is happening?"

"Yes," stated Simone, "We have worked out all the details, but only if you accept. Also, I'm willing to start you out at 55k because I know we will gain an asset. Take all the time you need and let me know if you are interested in my offer."

Leilani could barely hold back her smile as she shook Simone's hand. "I'd love that. Thank you so much. No, I do not need to think this over. If you will have me, I would love to join the team."

Leilani stood near the back of the conference room, still holding the folder in her hand like it might vanish if she let it go. Simone—graceful, poised, and the kind of woman who filled a space without raising her voice—had just finished shaking her hand.

"This is wonderful news," Simone had said, eyes warm with sincerity. "Please, call me Simone—and here's all my contact information. Reach out to me on Monday, and I'll email you the full onboarding details. Welcome to the team. I can't wait to see what skills you bring to the team."

And just like that, she was gone, her heels clicking confidently down the hall, leaving Leilani blinking in awe.

She stepped out of the room like she was walking through a dream, sunlight spilling across the polished floor. Her phone was already in her hand. Her heart raced, a grin tugging at her lips as she scrolled through her contacts.

No Marquise to call.

And honestly, that felt like a sense of peace.

She thought briefly of her cousin Maeve, who she knew would scream and dance on FaceTime, but in that moment, she needed something else first.

She needed to hear Chemistry's voice.

Before doubt could creep in, she tapped his name. It rang twice.

"Leilani," he answered, his voice warm and familiar.

Her breath caught in her throat for just a second. "Hey," she said, her voice soft but glowing. "Are you busy? I've got something to tell you."

"No, What's up?"

"I got it," she said, the words rushing out on a smile. "The internship. A real project management firm. Simone just offered it to me."

There was a pause on the line. The good kind—the kind where someone is grinning ear to ear and just trying to find the right words.

"That's dope as hell," he finally said, his voice lighting up. "I knew it. I *knew* you had it in you."

His excitement hit her like a rush of sun through clouds—bright, absolute, and unwavering.

Her smile deepened. "Thank you," she said, voice dipping into something softer, steadier. "I... I wanted this."

"And you earned it. Every bit of it."

She didn't say anything for a second, just let herself feel it—his belief in her, so full and clear it made her eyes sting.

"Where are you at?" he asked. "We're celebrating."

She laughed lightly, joy bubbling up in her chest. "Still downtown."

"Stay there," he said, his voice dropping into something low and specific. "I'm on my way."

Her heart pounded as she ended the call, and something settled in her chest.

There *was* someone to call now.

And this time, it felt like home.

******

After a few deep breaths, she opened her phone again and tapped Maeve's name. FaceTime rang three times before her cousin's glowing face filled the screen.

"Girl! What's up?" Maeve beamed. "You look like you've got a secret!"

Leilani couldn't hold it in. "I got it, Mae. The internship. I got it, and Mr. Taylor gave his blessing. Hell, I think he was the one who set up all of this goodness."

Maeve let out a scream, jumping back from the camera. "SHUT UP! Shut your entire face! Leilani, I *told* you! But damn, where did this VP come from? You didn't tell me you got this sort of pull. You better go!"

Leilani laughed, tears slipping down her cheeks before she could stop them. "I didn't think—"

"Don't you even finish that sentence?" Maeve cut in. "You did that. Getting the VP on your side without even trying or noticing. All those late nights, that stress, the boss from hell—you earned this. I'm so proud of you I could cry, but I'm gonna save my tears 'cause I'm wearing lashes."

They both laughed, the kind of laugh that felt like a release, like joy too immense to contain.

"I'm celebrating tonight," Leilani said. "Chemistry is on his way to meet me downtown."

"Oooh, now, who is this man?" Maeve teased, fanning herself. "You didn't tell me you tossed that trash, Marquise, to the curb. Baby, I can't wait until you tell me all about him; lord knows I need to hear some good news about a man when it comes to you. I gotta meet the man making my cousin leave that lame alone, yes baby!"

Leilani smiled, heart full. "I will tell you all about him. Plus, you and I have to go out for drinks, on me, because I'm getting a raise. Baby, she is giving me a high-earning salary. I owe you for helping me get stronger, girl."

"Girl, stop it. I will always be here for you. And you know I'm never going to turn down a free drank or meal. You know I love to eat. Now go enjoy this moment," Maeve said, her voice softening. "You deserve every bit of it. And make sure you call me tomorrow so we can plan outfits for your first day."

"I will. I promise."

As the call ended, Leilani stood on the sidewalk, sun warming her face, a new chapter unfolding beneath her feet.

She was ready. She was prepared for something new.

*

Rooftop Lounge Drama

They settle at a rooftop lounge downtown—twinkling string lights overhead, a jazz band playing low in the corner, the city skyline stretching behind them.

Chemistry wore dark denim, a crisp jacket, and some nice-fitting jeans. He also wore some nice Jordans, even though Leilani did not care much for them. Smiling widely with a nice set of bright white teeth, he was so excited that she wanted to celebrate with him. He was going to make the best of it.

"Look at you," he said, pulling her into a warm hug. "All official and glowing. I should've brought balloons."

Leilani laughed, cheeks flushing. "Don't tempt me. I'd wear a crown right now." Leilani was still wearing the outfit she had worn to the seminar. She was sexy in anything she wore, so she didn't need to change; she was dressed for the occasion.

They ordered drinks and toasted with sparkling glasses. She told him everything about Angela, and how Mr. Taylor had hinted at the opportunity, and how it had all felt like a dream.

He listened to her conversation the way he always did—fully present, like every word mattered.

But they weren't alone.

Marquise sat at the far end of the rooftop bar, nursing a drink by himself. He hadn't expected to see her or even wanted to be there. He just needed some time away from his wife and all the fake social media attention. But his whole body went still when he spotted her laughing, hand resting on Chemistry's arm.

He watched from a distance, unable to tear his eyes away.

The way she looked now—lit from within, easy, alive—was different from the version of her he remembered. This wasn't a woman waiting to be chosen.

She had already chosen herself.

And someone else had shown up to celebrate her for it.

Marquise tightened his grip around his glass, jaw clenching as he watched them toast again. For the first time, he wasn't a part of the moment.

He was watching it from the outside.

He was outside her world.

And it was killing him.

He started getting angrier the longer he watched. Each laugh, each clink of glasses, each lean-in moment between them scraped against something bitter and fragile inside him. That should've been him. That used to be him.

Before he realized what he was doing, he was on his feet.

He moved through the crowd and straight to their table.

"Leilani."

She turned slowly, her smile fading as her eyes landed on him. Chemistry sat next to her.

"What are you doing here?" she asked.

"I could ask you the same thing," Marquise said, voice low but laced with tension. "You out here celebrating like you couldn't hit me up to celebrate. I have been here through everything. I should have been the first person you called if you had any news. That's crazy, you would do me like this."

Chemistry stood now, calm but sharp. "Ay, my guy, you got about three seconds to back the fuck up or the energy gone change in this bitch." Usually, there wasn't any talking, but he was not about to let that aggressive energy show around Leilani too quickly.

Leilani placed a hand on Chemistry's chest, trying to keep things from boiling, but her voice was steel. "You don't get to speak on my joy. Not tonight. Not ever again. There would be no reason to call you about my good news. You didn't care about my goals anyway. You need to cut the bullshit.

"You gon act like that?" Marquise's voice rose. "Like we ain't got history? Could he ever understand you like I do? What you think he cares about you? You out here, fake kicking it with a complete stranger, come on now."

Chemistry took a step forward, his smile gone. "History doesn't mean shit. If you treated her like a chapter, you could skim through. Plus, you don't know me nigga so don't speak on me and my actions "

Leilani didn't flinch. She just wanted Marquise to move the fuck around. I don't understand why he thinks this shit is cool she thought to herself.

"You had your chance, Marquise," she said, voice clear and commanding. "And you wasted it. So, save whatever you think you're trying to do right now."

"Yo back the fuck up, and I'm not going keep saying it," Chemistry added, eyes hard now. "If I have to repeat myself, Ima beat the shit outa of you."

It was only then, when Marquise stepped back, face twisted with emotion, that he heard the familiar voice behind him.

"Marquise?"

He turned to see his wife standing there, confusion written all over her face, her phone still in her hand.

*

She had followed him and now she was caught in the middle of his bullshit chasing down this ugly ass girl.

The rooftop went quiet around them.

"This shit is messy as hell, and I love it. Let me start recording," a customer stated.

"I'm trying to see a fight!" another customer screamed.

And Leilani? She just picked up her glass, looked at chemistry, and smiled as if nothing touched her anymore.

The rooftop lounge had gone from an ambient and romantic setting to an electric and chaotic one in the blink of an eye. Glasses clinked in the background, but all eyes were now on Leilani, Chemistry, Marquise, and the woman who had just interrupted the night with venom in her voice.

Marquise's wife stormed through the crowd, eyes zeroed in on her husband. "Marquise, really muthafucka? Did you follow her here? This ugly ass bitch? Why are you so obsessed with this girl? What is it about her? Are you somehow too good for our money now nigga"

People from the crowd started yelling out. "Damn, she didn't have to do all that is she mad at her triflin' ass husband or the woman she foul. What the hell is he thinking? She is not wife material. A wife is seen, not heard; what the fuck are we doing? "One man said.

His wife is desperate, though. Who has to follow her husband? Maybe he doesn't want yo mean duck lookin ass. But who is the other girl? She is calm and collected? She doesn't seem to be worried about him or his wife; she is clearly on a date with a fine-looking man. That's the shit I need to get on. Said another female customer.

Amelia and her girls were cracking up at the show in front of them. They are usually the problem wild as hell shit; Tessa was just about to go ham on the waiter because she was bored. That bitch!

Amelia really couldn't say anything, though, because if it weren't Tessa, it would be one of the other girls from the clique.

Chemistry stood, already tense. Leilani remained seated, calm in the face of the storm.

"I should've known," his wife hissed. "I saw the way you looked at her. Even when we were supposed to be taking those damn influencer couple photos. You were obsessed. This ugly ass hoe doesn't got shit on me. This is what you want, Marquise, she's better than me, motherfucker. I have carried ya ass for years now!"

Then her attention snapped to Leilani. "And you? You're proud of this? Proud of being a husband-stealing side chick? You couldn't get your own man, so you circled back and tried to ruin my home?" I'm the prize, baby. I got what you want a life, a husband, and beautiful children bitch. You could never.

Leilani's brow barely lifted. She sipped her drink before answering. "You should be having this conversation with *your husband*. Not me."

Marquise was thinking that his wife was on straight bullshit.

Monica came here intending to let them both know who the fuck she was. Monica is not to be played with, and NO one, I mean NO ONE, will fuck with my bag she thought! Fuck his happiness. I need mine at all times, and he has been slacking. We gone set some shit straight today!"

"Don't act like you're innocent. I know women like you—always quiet, always sweet, waiting around to slip into somebody else's life like smoke under a door. Do you like to use a married man for his money? What you don't know is we fund our life; you won't be cutting into my ends like some damn homeless person. Bitch, as of right now, your little allowance is cut off. You're pathetic."

Chemistry took a step forward, voice low but dangerous. "Like my girl said, you need to be talking to your husband."

At that moment, Marquise and Leilani looked at Chemistry when he made that statement. Leilani felt butterflies in her stomach, but she looked over at Marquise, who looked at her like she was his girl.

What the fuck is going on? he thought, his face disgusted and hurt. I know she isn't with this guy, not this soon. No, she is still mine, he thought to himself.

Leilani stood up and raised her hand to stop Chemistry from getting confrontational. Something told her he did not need any police presence.

"You're angry. I get that. But don't confuse my silence with shame." She was now facing the woman fully. "He chased me. Lied to both of us. But I'm not the one who broke your vows—and I'm not the one still trying to convince me to stay. I told him we are done, and he won't take the hint. So now that you are here with us, why don't you help me?"

All you could hear was laughter from the crowd. "Baby, leave that grown-ass woman alone. She is not to be played with." One woman said.

"Let that woman have a good time with that fine-ass man damn! They stay trying to ruin a good night hatin asses! It looks like they were having a good time, too. She is ruining the vibes in this bitch." Said a couple talking loudly.

***

Security was already weaving through the crowd, gently guiding the wife and Marquise toward the exit as she continued shouting insults into the air.

Leilani turned to Chemistry, who gave her a slow, impressed nod. "You good?" he asked.

"Yeah," she said, letting out a long breath. "Better than ever."

They both returned to their table, and the energy around them shifted.

The crowd no longer saw drama. They saw a woman who chose peace—and meant it.

"Come on," Chemistry said softly. "Let's get outta here."

As security stepped in to manage the rooftop commotion, Leilani didn't look back. She let Chemistry lead her out, his hand firm on the small of her back, her steps unshaken.

Downstairs, the city night air greeted them like a reset button. Chemistry exhaled hard, then looked at her.

"You good?"

She nodded slowly. "Yeah. I'm good."
He searched her face for a moment, like he didn't fully believe her but respected her enough not to press.

"You handled that like a queen," he finally said. "Kept your crown the whole time."

She gave a tired smile. "I'm not trying to be royalty. I want peace."

"You earned it. All of it."

They walked in silence for a few blocks before ducking off into a loud bar, the music thicker than the air between them: the dim lighting, jazz in the background, and the comfort of quiet company. Leilani's phone buzzed nonstop, but she ignored it. She didn't need the internet's opinion.

She needed clarity.

Chemistry was laughing at something a bartender said, half-turned away, and for a split second, the scene warped for her. However, what she didn't know was that Chemistry popped into this bar quickly because one of his customers needed to re-up. She had texted him during all the chaos because she required more product due to the bar being packed tonight.

The laughter wasn't meant for her. He was slipping away, smiling into a world she couldn't reach. The familiar panic bloomed in her chest like wildfire. *He's going to leave too.* Her heart thudded so hard it hurt.

She hated how quickly her mind could betray her — how even now, with a man who had never given her reason to doubt, the old wounds made her flinch like a stray dog.

She backed up a step, bumping into a stool. She barely noticed when a glass clattered to the floor nearby.

And then —

Chemistry's hand closed around hers.

Firm. Steady. Real.

He turned toward her fully, anchoring her with his eyes. "*I'm right here,*" he said, just like he had seen the storm gather in her without her saying a word.

Leilani felt her ribs unlock, one by one, like a rusted gate creaking open.

She squeezed his hand back. Maybe, for once, she could believe it.

She looked across the table. "Mr. Taylor emailed me."

Chemistry raised an eyebrow. "Yeah?"

"He wants to meet for coffee. Said he wants to run something by me."

Chemistry leaned back in his chair, studying her. "He is offering an opportunity?"

"Shit, I don't know. He just sent me an email, but I figured it's gone be about that stupid ass Marquise's situation."

An evil expression appeared on Chemistry's face. "I promise if that lame ass dude messed up your opportunity, I'm going to fuck his bum ass up. I can't believe this shit, "he stated with a scowl.

"I know." She said, "But don't worry about it. One thing is for sure: I will be okay. Marquise is no longer running anything over here. I'm done with his ass, him and that weird wife of his. Can you believe she said she was going to stop my allowance?".

"Like bitch, are you crazy I've been paying for your family for years. He has not given me shit just always had his damn hand out, asshole.

"Damn," Chemistry laughed, "you going ham? You finally tired of that lame, huh?"

"He just wasted so much of my time, and I thought this was his love language. That is what keeps me angry when I think of him, because I thought we were building something special. His lame ass wife can think what she wants because I don't need him; little does she know. I was carrying our relationship and their entire household the fuck."

Chemistry leaned forward. "Leilani. You didn't just survive all this—you grew. You showed up. And you're still standing. That lame means nothing at this point, just dust flying in the wind. You're better than that, always have been."

"Go to that coffee meeting with the VP. You never know; it could be great news. I'm always rooting for ya, smart, beautiful lady."

She smiled, hard, her face flushing, her breath hitching in her chest. "You always know what to say."

He reached across the table and laced his fingers through hers. "That's 'cause I see you."

And this time, she didn't flinch. Didn't question it. She just held his hand and let herself believe it was okay to be seen.

He was peeping the scene, and the bartender let him know she was good to go. So, Chemistry got up so they could leave. His business was done.

Leilani followed him outside the bar.

The car door shut with a soft click, sealing Leilani inside, surrounded by silence and the weight of her thoughts. Chemistry slid into the driver's seat, his hands resting on the wheel, but he didn't start the car right away. The streetlights cast long shadows across the dashboard, flickering across his face, calm, unreadable, waiting.

Leilani stared down at her hands, fingers twisting together in her lap. The words were bubbling up, tripping over each other, desperate to fill the silence before it swallowed her whole.

"I'm sorry," she blurted out, her voice too loud in the stillness. "I didn't know he'd be there. I didn't — I swear I'm not — I didn't mean for any of that to happen."

Chemistry didn't say anything right away. He let her words hang in the air, heavy and trembling, like they were begging him to either catch them or let them fall.

She rushed to fill the space. "I'm not that type of woman — I'm not messy like that. I should've told you about him, I just — I thought it was over, I thought I could leave it behind. I didn't think—"

"Leilani." His voice was soft, but firm. Enough to make her stop mid-breath.

He turned toward her, the streetlight catching in his eyes, making them gleam. "You don't owe me an explanation for your past. But I do need to know something."

Her stomach clenched. "What?"

"Are you done with him? For real."

The question was simple, but it cracked something inside her wide open. She wanted to say yes — hell, she needed to say yes — but her voice caught in her throat. Not because she still wanted Marquise, but because **HE** had been her entire world for so long. Letting him go meant letting go of the version of herself who thought love meant **saving someone, sacrificing for someone, disappearing for someone.**

"I'm done." Her voice was quiet, but steady. "I swear to you, I'm done. But what was that about in the restaurant, I'm your girl now," she teased.

Chemistry watched her for a beat longer, as if he was weighing her words, deciding if they held the truth, not just for him, but for herself too.

He laughed. "I don't know what came over me, and I apologize; I should not have overstepped. I didn't like how they both tried to double-team you as if you were there alone. I don't like that kind of bullying."

"But at that moment, I saw a strong, graceful woman, my woman, so it came out that way. We don't have to talk about that right now. I just wanted to let that lame-ass nigga know it may not be his choice in a minute. He can keep trying to use your emotions against you, not realizing you could be a different woman now," he said confidently.

"As long as you say you're done, I believe you." He finally nodded, starting the car. "Then let's go celebrate your win and leave that trash where it belongs."

The corners of her mouth twitched, the ghost of a smile tugging at her lips, even as her fingers kept twisting in her lap. "I'm sorry."

"Stop apologizing." His hand reached across the console, palm up, waiting. "You're good with me."

She stared at his hand for a second before finally sliding her own into it. His fingers curled around hers, warm and solid — nothing like the grasping, needy touch she was used to. This wasn't possession. This was **present.**

For the first time in a long time, she felt **seen.**

As the car pulled away from the curb, Leilani glanced back through the window — one last time — at the restaurant, the ghost of her old life fading into the distance.

She faced forward again, her fingers still resting in Chemistry's palm, and let herself believe, just for a moment, that maybe — just maybe — she deserved something **more.**

*

Fresh Grounds, Fresh Perspective

The soft hum of conversation, the clink of glasses, and the scent of grilled food filled the air as Leilani sat across from Chemistry at a small table tucked in the corner of a lively rooftop bar. String lights hung overhead, casting a golden glow across the tables, and for the first time in a long time, Leilani felt... light.

"I hope we don't have any more problems. Chem, really another rooftop bar. Leilani laughed, admiring chemistry from across the table.

"Naw," he stated. "We are in a better environment where it feels like home."

This was chemistry, spot low-key. He owns everything, including the parking lot outside, but this could be something they can explore later. Right now, he just wanted to get to know her better and ensure she has a better night."

It surprised her how easily she could sit there with him. There was no tension pulling her shoulders tight or calculating her every word. She was also grateful that she didn't need to watch what she said because people always wanted to make something out of nothing. It felt nice to talk, relax, and get to know one another. Chemistry sat back in his chair, one arm draped casually over the back, his drink in his other hand, looking entirely at ease, like they belonged there, like they'd done this a hundred times.

"So, what's the official title for your new role? He asked, raising an eyebrow. "I knew you were going to lock something in. You already looked so confident and professional at the seminar. I thought you were a speaker at the event.

Leilani smiled, the kind of smile that reached her eyes. "Project Management Intern. Nothing fancy. "And, me," Leilani said, pointing at herself, "speaking at the seminar, no way I am there to learn.

Chemistry tilted his head. "Nah, see, I don't like that. That's not enough sauce. You'll be out here running the show before the year's out — they don't know it yet."

She laughed, the sound bubbling out before she could catch it. "You're giving me a promotion already? Well, since you mentioned it, I was recommended by one of the VPs from my current job. I had no idea he was paying attention to me. I assumed he just believed that my boss did all his work. He put in a good word for me to my new boss, and apparently, he is willing to offer me a severance package."

"Damn right." He leaned forward, elbows on the table, his voice dropping slightly lower. "But wait, are you serious about doing your boss's work. And how the fuck did the VP find out? Shorty, yo job is wild as hell. Woman, help me understand this madness.

Leilani burst out laughing so hard. This caught her off guard because she is not used to a man cracking jokes. She was playful, but had to internalize that playfulness in her last relationship. She would never have imagined a situation where her mate could be just as goofy as her.

Marquise hated it when she joked all the time, saying, "I'm too busy for jokes; my only concern is getting to the money." Leilani thought to herself the only money that ass hole was getting was mines.

"Well, I can try and answer some of your questions," she laughed. Yes, I have been doing my boss's job for almost three years. I have a strong drive to understand the details and use that understanding to improve the company. I enjoy analyzing various budgets for different projects. This will help me determine which project is better equipped to increase the company's yearly revenue." She smiled, just thinking about all the great work she had done over the years. It's nothing her boss can ever take from her.

Chemistry sat there, listening intently to her story, not interrupting, and taking pleasure in the passion and determination on her face. Seeing her talk about something she is so passionate about was genuinely cute. This woman is brilliant, and I admire her determination.

"And I have no idea how the VP got involved. I didn't tell anyone but my cousin Maeve that I was attending the seminar. No one at my job knew this. One day, after a frustrating meeting with my boss, who was taking the credit once again. I just went for it."

"Mr. Taylor, the VP," she laughed, because why am I calling him the VP? "He randomly approached my desk and asked if I would walk with him. Now, as you can imagine, I was nervous as hell. Like, what does he want with me?"

"Yeah, I get that," said Chemistry. "Like damn, are you sure you looking for me? Let me get the boss for you. He stated, laughing.

"Yes, she said that was really my thought process, like naw you're not looking for me." They laughed and went back and forth, wondering what Mr. Taylor was on.

"Let me finish!" she laughed, holding her sides from laughing. "Fine, go on. I will stop for the moment," said Chemistry.

"Mr. Taylr started by saying, "Hey, I heard you are attending the seminar downtown. Now imagine the surprise on my face because, like I said, I didn't want them to know at work. But he told me he had his sources. He also said someone would approach me about an opportunity, and I should highly consider the offer."

"Well, it came down to the last second, and I felt like at the time that no one would approach me. Then, this lovely lady approached and told me about an internship in project management. She even informed me about my starting pay, which is higher than what I'm currently receiving. I don't know why I'm telling you everything, but I trust you like I have known you my whole life.

"We have known each other; we just had to find our way back to one another," he winked, looking over at her. "You also don't know if we met in another past life," Chemistry said with a bright, confident smile.

"Man, shorty, you got some good energy about yaself. I rarely entertain women because many females are up to no good. But I love that you have aspirations and dreams that you want to complete. That's different from where I come from. It's not too many people I see like you every day."

This made him notice not only that he liked what was in front of him, but also that her mind was extraordinary. "I see you, Leilani. You've been holding up the weight of other people's dreams for so long that you forgot you had your own. But you're stepping into them now. That's a big deal."

Her chest tightened, that mix of pride and vulnerability making her feel exposed and empowered. "I'm not used to anyone seeing me like that. You have so many wonderful things to say. You just met me and have more faith in me than many people."

"Well," Chemistry said, sitting back again with a slight smirk, "get used to it. It's also not every day I come across a person like you. You inspire me to reach goals I never thought of before. And remember, I see the potential, not vice versa." He laughed

She sipped her drink to hide the warmth spreading across her face. "You're always this confident? And thank you for your comments on inspiration. That's all I ever wanted to be. I love to inspire people to do better and push themselves. I know I need to take my advice, but I'm getting there," she smiled.

He gave her a slow, deliberate once-over. "Only when I'm right. And yes, that's the energy you give off. It's electrifying like a mouthafucka, and it seems to me like you're already taking your advice," he laughs.

Her laugh came easier this time, less guarded and more natural. She felt herself unfolding, piece by piece, as if she were remembering how to exist outside of survival mode. She told him about her awkward first meeting with the CEO of her current job—how she almost tripped over the welcome mat—and Chemistry cracked up, calling her "Ms. Grace Under Pressure."

They swapped stories—nothing too heavy, just enough to let their personalities dance together. He told her about a time he accidentally sent a client to a project to start helping feed the poor. He was setting up to supply a bigger hood, which meant more money for him. However, the nigga he sent was super scary, so he had to come smooth things over.

Chemistry gave her his version of the story. "I sent one of the team members to set up new opportunities within a low-income area. However, something went wrong and I had to come and intervene so the people from the neighborhood wouldn't beat his ass. Leilani and Chemistry started laughing until it felt like their sides ached.

However, Leilani did not know he was talking about a situation from his street dealings.

The breeze carried the scent of night-blooming jasmine across the rooftop, and for once, Leilani wasn't waiting for the other shoe to drop. She was just… there. In the moment. With him.

"You know," she said, swirling the ice in her glass, "I didn't think I'd be laughing tonight."

Chemistry held her gaze, something softer in his expression now. "That's 'cause you never had somebody around who knew how to make you feel safe enough to laugh."

Her throat tightened again, but this time, it wasn't fear. It was the unfamiliar weight of being cared for, without having to earn it, beg for it, or pay for it.
"Thank you," she said softly.

"For what?"

"For this. For not making me feel like I must be anything other than myself. And showing me a good time after the night we just had. A normal man would have run off and cut their losses."

"Well, I'm not like normal people, shorty. I know gold when I see it, and I won't let you get away too fast. Chemistry raised his glass. "To you — the real you."

She clinked her glass against his, and for the first time in forever, she believed there might be a version of herself worth celebrating.

The night air had cooled, and the rooftop crowd had thinned as the city settled into its quieter hours. Leilani and Chemistry stayed put, their drinks half-empty, and their conversation slowed into something softer, more intimate.

Leilani leaned her elbow on the table, chin resting lightly on her hand. "You make it sound easy," she said, her voice low but clear.

"What's that?" Chemistry's eyes stayed on her, the streetlights reflecting like liquid gold.

"Letting go of old stuff. Old versions of yourself, old fears. Old... people."

He didn't answer immediately, letting the silence stretch between them, like he knew she needed the space to say it aloud.

"It's not easy," he finally said. "It's work. Sometimes it's ugly work. But you gotta decide who's worth that work — and most times, it's not them." His gaze softened. "It's you."

She looked down at her fingers, tracing the condensation on her glass. "I don't think I ever felt worth it."

Chemistry reached across the table, his fingers brushing hers. Not grabbing, not demanding — just a touch, just enough to remind her she wasn't alone in that space.

"That's 'cause you've been loving people who couldn't even see you," he said. "People who only see what you do for them, not who you are."

Leilani's throat tightened, tears pressing at the edges of her vision. But she didn't cry. Not here. Not in front of him.

"I see what you can do, Leilani." His voice was low, but firm. "I have seen it from the first moment we bumped into each other."

Her heart stuttered at the ease with which he said it, like it was a simple truth and not some grand declaration. She wasn't accustomed to being seen without having to fight for it.

"Can I ask you something?" she said, her voice barely above a whisper.

"Anything."

"Why are you being so nice to me?" There was no accusation in her tone, just raw curiosity like she couldn't quite believe she was allowed to have someone on her side without earning it.

Chemistry leaned back, stretching his arms across the back of his chair, considering her question like it was worth an honest answer.

"'Cause I see something in you," he said. "Strength, you don't even know you've got. I know what it's like to come out of some shit and not recognize yourself. I've been there. And I don't know — maybe I like seeing you realize how dope you are."

She let out a shaky laugh. "You don't even know me."

"I'm getting there," he said, giving her that signature smirk. "And so far, I like what I see."

She didn't know how to respond, so she didn't. She just sat with it, letting herself feel something beyond doubt for once. It was foreign and terrifying, but it wasn't bad.

The ride home was quiet but not awkward. Chemistry had one hand on the wheel, the other resting on his thigh, his fingers tapping some silent rhythm. Leilani stared out the window, the city lights blurring past, her thoughts tumbling in a way that felt... less heavy. Like maybe the weight wasn't hers to carry alone anymore.

When he pulled up in front of her building, he didn't rush to say goodbye. "You gonna be alright?" he asked.

Leilani smiled softly. "Yeah. I think so."
"Good." He paused, then added, "I meant what I said — you can call me. Anytime."

She nodded, stepping out of the car. As she walked up to her door, she could feel his eyes on her, not in a hungry, possessive way she was used to, but in a way that made her think... am I worth looking at?

******

Inside, she kicked off her heels, collapsing onto her bed without turning on the lights. Her phone vibrated on the nightstand, and the screen lit up with Marquise's name again. And again.

The first message was a string of question marks.

The next, **"Where are you at???"**

Then, **"You think you're slick, huh?"**
And then the voice-mails started — all left in quick

succession, his voice shifting from confused to angry to pleading.

She didn't pay them any mind after listening and then erasing them. Awww, poor baby. What those feelings hurt! Now he knows how I feel, but not really. I don't have no damn kids she thought. He and his wife did the most tonight; shit is crazy. I need to call Maeve and get her up to speed but fuck it, I will call her tomorrow. I'm tired, she thought. It had been a long fucking day.

She rolled onto her back, staring at the ceiling, and let her mind drift back to Chemistry — his voice, his touch, the way he didn't demand anything from her but her truth.

For the first time in a long time, she fell asleep with her phone face down, her heart light, and her mind full of possibility.

*

Unexpected Attention

It was the next day at work, and Leilani had been busy since she came into this bitch. Her boss had been issuing orders since he arrived. And yes, he came after her, but had other shit to do: miss me with that.

She also emailed her new employer, requesting the necessary paperwork to initiate the onboarding process. Simone, her new boss, sent all the paperwork, and she plans to complete it by the end of the day. She has had enough of this job and her boss.

However, she was still on cloud nine after her date with chemistry. Leiani was so busy she couldn't take a break, let alone call her cousin Maeve yet. She figured she would work through the morning and then call her for lunch.

By noon, she was drowning in multiple requests from Mr. Harding. I don't care what he says. It's lunch time, damn. She locked her computer and saw several missed calls and texts from her cousin Maeve. She also noticed that her social media inboxes were flooded.

Her phone is always on silent when she is at work. Plus, nobody calls or texts her except Marquise. Ugh, and I don't have time for that garbage right now.

A DM from someone she hadn't talked to since college asking, *"Is that you in the rooftop video?"* She had seen some messages from her coworker that has walked past her desk all day; they were also asking her about the event. What the hell is going on? Let me call Mae.

But the message that stopped her cold?

Mr. Taylor

Subject: Coffee?

"Saw the clip. You handled yourself more poise than most executives I know and collaborate with.

Let's grab coffee later this week—I want to run something by you.

Keep shining, Leilani. You've got people paying attention now. The right ones."

She reread it twice. This wasn't just a moment anymore. It was leverage.

She closed her laptop, heart steady.

Let them talk. Let them guess. Let them pretend they know what's going on with her life. Leilani was not about to respond to random people or people she didn't talk to in the office.

Just because people are starting to see her, she needs to eat up all the attention. Naw, I'm not that hard up for it, I'm beginning to love myself.

She grabbed her jacket and keys. She was headed to Maeve's Apartment to catch up. All this shit was crazy, and she had no idea that it had gone completely viral. She does not hang out on social media; she keeps it for when she wants to be nosy.

Leilani sat cross-legged on Maeve's couch, took her blazer off, and had her coffee mug in hand—the same viral video was playing on loop on Maeve's phone.

"Check this shit out no this part right here—" Maeve scrubbed the video back five seconds, her voice high with excitement, "—where you said, 'This is the last time you will ever ruin a moment meant for me' and then walked away like you didn't just shut that man *and* his wife down? ICONIC."

Leilani groaned, burying her face in her hands. "Please stop watching it."

"No. Absolutely not. You are the internet's new favorite heroine," Maeve said, sipping her matcha latte with extra drama. "Girl, you had the rooftop bar *jumping*. And Chemistry? The way he stood up like he was about to throw hands?"

"I thought he might actually fight him," Leilani muttered. It was supposed to be our first date, and it went quickly."

"Because he doesn't look like the type to let anybody disrespect people that is with him. He looks like he would beat the hell out of somebody. You need to see if he got a friend for me." Maeve said. "When I look at the video, he's already locked in with you. Protective mode activated. Also, let's talk about Marquise's wife—where did *she* come from?"

Leilani shook her head. "She followed him, following me there. The whole thing was... surreal."

"Well, she dared to call *you* a homewrecker. Like she doesn't live in denial with a man that's emotionally obsessed with someone else?"

"Mae."

"No, I'm serious," Maeve said, eyes narrowed. "The way she came at you. The jealousy and the projection were giving rise to a real feeling: 'I've lost already, but I want one last swing.' She saw you shining and couldn't take it."

Leilani sighed, staring into her coffee. "I don't like the attention. I didn't ask for any of this."

"Maybe not," Maeve said, scooting closer, "but you *deserved* to be seen. And now that people *are* seeing you? Let 'em. They're watching a woman who refused to shrink."

Leilani looked over, heart soft. "Thanks, Mae."

Maeve winked. "Now, go meet with that executive. You don't know what he wants to talk about. Your glow-up is not just personal—it's professional too."

Leilani laughed, which started in the chest and lingered in the throat. "You're the best hype woman alive, " she said, getting up and walking towards the door.
"I love you, cousin. Make sure you do the damn thing today."

"I love you, too," Leilani said, closing the door behind her. She was ready for this meeting; she had a good feeling about it, but meeting up didn't mean she wasn't nervous.

**

Leilani jumped in her car and went to meet Mr. Taylor. He happened to send her another email, asking if she was free to meet today. He asked her not to return to the office but to come and meet him instead.

So now she was on her way to see what he would like to talk about. Hollis Ridge had a popular, quiet corner café behind the local dentist's office—one of those places with warm lighting, worn leather chairs, and playlists that knew when to let the silence speak.

Mr. Taylor was already there when she arrived, standing to greet her with that same calm, unreadable expression he always wore in boardrooms.

"Leilani," he said with a nod, gesturing to the seat across from him. "Thanks for making time."

"Of course," she replied, setting her bag down. "I appreciate the invitation."

After they ordered, there was a pause—easy, not awkward. Mr. Taylor studied her for a moment, then leaned in slightly.

"You know that video will outlive the news cycle, right?"

She smiled faintly. "So, I've been told."

"Good. I do appreciate how you handled yourself. That was real leadership. Controlled, grounded, clear. Not many people, especially under pressure, could've held themselves with that much respect."

Leilani tilted her head. "I wasn't trying to lead anything. I just... refused to let anyone steal that moment from me. Plus, the history behind that is an entire mess."

Mr. Taylor smiled. "That's exactly what made it powerful."

He sipped his espresso, then set the cup down carefully. "Listen. I reached out to you because my contact at the new firm informed me that you have accepted the offer.

"Yes: she stated, "I have you to thank. I appreciate you putting in such a good word for me." She smiled and looked over at him.

"The hardest thing about this is losing such a great worker. You have been a valuable asset to us for the last few years. I know it has been tough, maybe doing more than what's expected of you, but I have seen you over the years.

"I have called you here to let you know you have my blessing. You deserve this and so much more. I am prepared to offer you a severance package of $12,750, and I would also like to cash out your accrued PTO. So, what do you think? "

Leilani was too shocked to speak. She had no idea this was what he wanted to meet for. Hell, yeah, she was going to take the job; she didn't know that someone so close had supported her. It's so crazy what can happen if you step outside the box, she thought!

"Oh my!" she stated. "Mr. Taylor, I have no idea what to say. Thank you so much for the severance package; I accept. This is amazing. Should I finish up the rest of the week?"

"Well, that is also another ask I have for you. Now, hear me out. What do you think of staying part-time for two weeks, depending on how long this takes? He thought.

"What do you mean by that, Mr. Taylor? What do I need to do? Would this affect my new job? I have already accepted the offer, and she has sent the onboarded paperwork.

"No, this will not affect your job offer. I have already talked to your new manager, and we are on the same page. Only if you agree, of course. We have known each other for years, so there's no need to worry. If you are willing, I would like you to look for and hire your new replacement."

"After this help, you are done with us. We have kept you from your dreams long enough. You deserve this, and I'm always here for you. Your hard work has paid off." He stated excitement!

"Leilani blinked. "You trust me to hire the new me? Wait, you trust me to do this? I would be so happy to help." She yelled excitedly. "I'm so sorry, this is just amazing news, but what about Mr. Hardling?"

"What about him? This is a request from me to ensure we attract the best talent. Why would I not trust someone who has been an asset? Anytime you have a problem with him, let me know."

"Yes, of course, I will help. Just let me look at the candidates."

"I knew you would say yes. I have already sent some resumes over to your email. Please set them up and choose your person. Also, I trust you have no reason to inform me during the process. Just alert me once you have chosen the winning person. I'll sponsor your choice personally."

Her heart skipped. "I thought this was just coffee."

"It is," Mr. Taylor said with a slight grin. "But you've earned more than caffeine, and congratulations." He states, toasting his cup of coffee with Leilani.

For a moment, she was silent, processing, holding the weight of what was being asked of her.

"You think I can do this?"

"I think you've been ready. You just needed the space to be you. I also wanted to apologize for everything you went through under Mr. Hardling."

Outside the café window, the city buzzed by, unbothered, unaware of the moment between a woman who once faded into the dark abyss of an empty school bus and then emerged into being with a man who saw her as something more than just a means to an end.

And this time, it's only about Leilani and what worked for her. And you know what?

She wasn't backing away.
*

Replacement Shopping

The next day, after their coffee session, Leilani sat across from Mr. Taylor in a sleek glass-walled conference room, the skyline behind him glowing in the early morning light.

"So, here's the next step," Mr. Taylor said. "The fact that you will leave the company will be announced later. It's nobody's business anyway, but in the meantime, I need *you* to get started on finding your replacement."

Your new boss is waiting to get her new asset. He laughed. "Well, that's what she keeps saying on our calls."

Leilani blinked. "Are you serious?" She could not stop asking, never would she think to be seen.

Mr. Taylor nodded. "You know the job better than anyone. I trust your instincts. You'll sit in on the interviews and have the final say. It's yours to shape."

Before she could fully respond, the door opened. Mr. Hardling stepped in, his smile tight and eyes already narrowed.

"Leilani? Interviewing?" he said, a touch too loud. "I assumed I'd be handling that."

Mr. Taylor stood slowly, polite but firm. "Mr. Hardling, thanks for joining. Yes, Leilani will be leading the candidate evaluation. With my full backing."

Hardling's jaw flexed. "With all due respect, she's leaving the company. Does her opinion matter since she officially has a new role? Shouldn't we leave decisions like this to the management that currently holds a position?"

"She *is* management," Mr. Taylor replied coolly. "And the fact that she knows the position, the workflow, and the blind spots makes her more qualified than anyone else in this building to choose who takes her place."

Leilani stayed silent, composed until Mr. Taylor turned to her.

"You fine with that?" he asked.

She nodded once. "Absolutely."

Hardling crossed his arms. "This is highly irregular."

"So was watching her do your job for the past two years," Mr. Taylor said, eyes never leaving Hardling. "Get used to it."

The room fell into a tense silence.

And for the first time, Leilani wasn't the one shrinking into the background.

She was at the head of the table—and this time, she was staying there. Rather, her old boss liked it or not, and she did not give a single fuck.

She looked over at him. Why does he look salty all of a sudden? She laughed to herself.

Everyone was enjoying lunch, but not Mr. Hardling. He was stewing, and he had just devised a plan of action.

Mr. Hardling sat at his desk, phone in hand, voice low and sharp as he spoke to a senior HR manager.

"I just don't think it's appropriate for Leilani to be making hiring decisions," he said. "She's already moved on. Her head's not in this department anymore."

"But Mr. Taylor asked her to lead the process," the HR manager said.

Hardling smiled coldly. Yes, well, Taylor has been out of touch with our department structure lately. We need someone experienced in leadership, not someone newly promoted off viral fame."

"Are you saying that Leilani is not qualified to conduct interviews? Are you also stating that she is being promoted due to popularity and not productivity?" the HR manager asked.

"Uh, Uh, Uh," he stammered. "I was just pointing out that this situation is not normal. For some reason, all of this is happening outside of the process. It's essential to have different management levels to make decisions of this importance. We have to make sure that the company keeps profiting."

He ended the call and immediately forwarded a few resumes of candidates he preferred—ones who were compliant, mediocre, and easy to mold. He even scheduled interviews behind Leilani's back.

But Mr. Taylor wasn't stupid. He just made sure to send them to Leilani. He wanted to see how this would play out. I shouldn't be testing Leilani, but this is good preparation for her next role. And if there's one thing I know, Leilani can handle herself. I noticed her work ethic over the past two years.

When she saw the forwarded invites, she didn't react emotionally; she laughed. "Fine, Mr. Hardling, if you want to go there, let's go."

Why not add some of his candidates? Let's shake it up.

Later on, that morning.

Leilani walked into the room in a tailored navy jumpsuit, heels clicking like punctuation marks. She held a folder of notes from top candidates in one hand, wore a calm smile, and had the best intentions at heart; she was in positive spirits.

Hardling was already there, standing stiffly with his arms crossed.

"Didn't know we'd be doubling up today," he said dryly.

Mr. Taylor replied smoothly, "We're not. Leilani's leading. You're assisting."

Leilani took her seat, flipped open her folder, and met Hardling's gaze head-on. "Let's begin," she said. Leilani sat comfortably in the HR conference room, her neatly prepared interview packets at hand.

She got up to bring in the first candidate, and as soon as she entered the doorway, she noticed an unfamiliar face at the table.

"Excuse me," she politely asked the woman. Are you here to interview for the coordinator position?
"

The woman smiled and nodded. "Yes, Mr. Hardling told me to come early. Said he'd be conducting the interview himself."

Leilani's brow lifted. Yasss, this is the energy I need right now. She thought to herself.

**

"Yes, of course. I was expecting you, and I'm excited to get to know you," she stated with a smile.

She guided the young lady into the conference room and showed her where to sit. Hardling looked around widely. He was not expecting Leilani to invite Misty so fast. He had to think fast; she was not qualified, and he was hoping to slide her in.

"Good morning," Leilani stated. "My name is Leilani, and I have recently moved on from this position. I will be interviewing with Mr. Hardling, the manager for this role.

Please answer the questions to the best of your ability, and we are happy to repeat any if needed. Please excuse the top of our heads as we will be taking notes during the interview."

Misty smiled and stated, "It's nice to meet you both; my name is Misty."

"Great, let's get started," said Leilani. "I will allow Mr. Hardling to take the first question."

"Sure," he said! Hardling thought I could make her look good, which would work great.

"You have special attention to detail. Please let me know how you would pay attention to details?"

"Yes, of course," she stammered. She looked over to Mr. Hardling for guidance. After all, he called and told her it was a sure thing.

"Uh, the way I would pay attention to details is to ensure I'm doing everything correctly," she said.

"Great answer, Misty." He did not want to push her too much, knowing she could only do what he told her.
"Great," Leilani stated, "I have the next question."

"Can you please tell me about a time when you helped ensure a project was organized with notes, and when you have this information, how was it stored?"

Misty looked off into the distance, unsure how to answer the question exactly, but then she remembered that she had worked at a beauty shop, where she had organized hair for some coins. Well, that was before she got fired for having sex with the owner's husband.

"Well, once, I gathered all the hair in the shop and ensured it was in the same place. The owners liked it so much that they also want me to separate by color."

Leilani looked at her and did not know what to say. Well, at least she understood the organizational part, which is a good thing.

"Thank you for your answer." She stated as she jotted down some notes.

Misty smiled. I'm doing great, she thought.

"I got the next question." Said Hardling. Tell me about a time when you could take tasks from your supervisor and apply them correctly."

She thought momentarily and said, "I would always take good notes and follow everything asked of me. I would not deviate from what my supervisor explicitly wants me to do."
"Great answer," said Mr. Hardling.

So, she is simply saying that she would not think outside the box and explore other opportunities that her supervisor is unaware of. I don't like it, Leilani thought.

"I have the last question, Misty," said Leilani with a soft smile.

"Tell me about a time when you had multiple tasks and what you did to prioritize them by importance?"

Misty was on a roll and believed that she was acing this interview. I got this shit in the bag, she thought.

"I would just ensure I know what is important for my boss. It's essential to understand what he needs and ensure those things are accurate. He would be the safe source for all things getting done," she said confidently.

Mr. Hardling smiled and winked at her. She is saying everything right, and I will do everything possible to ensure she gets the role. Nothing like Leilani. He could barely keep up with all the new things she was bringing to the table. Talk about exhausting, the only thing I will miss about her is that she made me look so good, he thought.

Meanwhile, Leilani sat in thought. She did not like this candidate and did not think she was a good fit for the role. This role needs a self-starter with a go-getter attitude. The top pick is a diligent researcher who seeks out opportunities that leaders might miss.

"Thank you, Misty. That wraps up our questions. Do you have any questions for us?" Leilani asked.

"Yeah," Misty stated. "How much do we get paid, and what are those vacation days looking like. This nice establishment would have to have some good benefits." She inquired with a raised eyebrow.

Mr. Hardling was taken aback because he had told her the deal before asking her to interview for the role.

This bitch is doing the most right now I told her to be cool and just let me take the lead."

"Oh, of course," Leilani smiled. "We have an excellent benefits package being offered for this role, starting at 35,000K and one week of vacation time that is set to reset every year.

"Yes, now that's what I'm talking about. But why do you need to reset the time every year? Can we keep the days from last year if we don't use them?"

"At this company, vacation days do not roll over at your level. You either use them or lose them. But every year on January 1, you get 1 week of vacation time for the year." Leilani smiled once she finished.

There was silence in the room for about 60 seconds.

Leilani cleared her throat and asked, "Did you have any more questions?".

"Oh no, that's all I wanted to know. Just tell me when I start."

This bitch thought Leilani. "We have a few more interviews to get through. However, we will contact you no matter what decision we make."

"Great," she said. Thank you both for your time, and I look forward to hearing from you!"

"Thank you," Both Mr. Hardling and Leilani said in unison.

With that, she left the building, waiting for them to get in touch with her. She knew she was getting the job. Now, she had to tell Big Mickey she had gotten a job and could pay for her freedom. She no longer wanted to sell her body; if she could secure a job like this, her life would change.

She walked to her car, clicking and clacking, smiling to herself. Man, my life is about to boss up, she smiled.

**

Back in the interview room, both parties were lost in thought.

Leilani thought there was no Way in hell she would cosign Misty. She did not possess the necessary qualities for this role.

While Mr. Hardling was thinking, he found an excellent replacement for Leilani. He believed that she would be better. He would no longer have to work with an overachiever, and he would have to explain things he had no clue about. His job was so hard with Leilani here, and he could not wait to be rid of her.

One by one, the real candidates filed in, each greeted by Leilani with professionalism and a sharp, practiced eye. She asked questions that cut through the fluff, tested emotional intelligence, and identified those who viewed the work as more than a checklist.

She saw bits of her old self in some of them and the mistakes of old leadership in others.

But by the end of the day, she didn't just have a favorite.

She had a vision to find the best person for the role.

And this time, no one—not even Mr. Hardling—could block it.

The next candidate walked in. Leilani was already captivated by her professionalism and confidence.

Ava walked in feeling super nervous. But she had been practicing for about a week and was ready. She had conducted thorough research on the company and believed she would be an excellent fit for the position.

"Good morning, my name is Leilani, and I have recently moved on from this position. I will be interviewing with the manager for this role, Mr. Hardling. "

Please answer the questions to the best of your ability. We are willing to repeat any question if needed. Please excuse the top of our heads; we will take notes."

Ava smiled politely and stated, "It's nice to meet you both. My name is Ava Tanner."

"Nice to meet you. Let's go ahead and get started," said Leilani. "I will allow Mr. Hardling to take the first question."

"Sure," he said! Let's get through this, I know who I want anyway! He thought.

"We need a person for this role with special attention to detail. Please describe when you had to pay special attention to details?"

"Sure thing," Ava smiled cheerfully. "At my last job, we had a project that had many details embedded into it. These many details were essential to the different managers. So, I took each manager's comments on which details were important. Then, I analyzed the project and determined when and where those details would arise. Once found, I alerted each manager and informed them about the project's completion, as well as how their details had contributed to shaping the process.

"I like that answer, but you could have added more depth." Mr. Hardling said he would do everything possible to make her look bad.

"That was a well-thought-out answer. I appreciated how you addressed the process if more than one manager was involved. We go through similar activities in the company," Leilani stated with a look of satisfaction. "I have the following question she sang out.

"Can you please tell me about a time when you helped ensure a project was organized with notes, and when you have this information, how was it stored?"

"Yes," stated Ava. "At my last internship, it was my job to ensure that all the proposal was organized and explained. I had to work with each division to refine their proposal for inclusion in the project. I took notes from each division and captured them on a SharePoint site. I granted access to all business units, ensuring they could not view the work of others. Once completed, I shared this link with the leaders so they could choose which proposal to proceed with. It was a good project because I talked to many people from different areas."

Leilani loved that answer: "Thank you so much for that answer. It shows that you value the opinions of others. You want to ensure that all business units had a say and that their work was well represented."

"I think that answer is too wordy, and why would you have to contact so many people? It seems like you stalled the project because so many were involved, but this structure does align with ensuring all parties were included."

Leilani rolled her eyes. I wish he would shut the fuck up. This girl is giving some of the best answers. I hope he doesn't drive her away with his cruel behavior. She thought as she jotted down some notes.

For some reason, Ava was nervous; this man did not like her. What is going on? She had prepared for this. But you know what fuck him? I will get through this interview. I came prepared, and I'm going to show them.

"I got the next question." Said Hardling. Tell me about a time when you could take tasks from your supervisor and apply them correctly."

She thought momentarily and said, "I would gather the list from my supervisor. Then, I would work on each task, ensuring I wasn't missing anything. I will also research the individual functions to determine if it has already been completed or if there is an opportunity to incorporate something new. If something new is found, I would set aside time for my supervisor and me to review it. Once completed, I will proceed with the tasks as discussed.

"I think you are missing the point of taking tasks from your supervisor. You would want to make sure you are following them to a tee; there is no room for interpretation," said Mr. Hardling.

Her answer is perfect to me. The top candidate would want to think outside the box and make sure they are researching alternative solutions. He is so annoying to me, she thought.

"I loved that answer. "Not only are you confirming that you will take the information from your supervisor, but you are also stating that you would research anything they may have missed, giving the company the best possible outcome."

"I have the last question, Ava," said Leilani with a soft smile.

"Tell me about a time when you had multiple tasks and what you did to prioritize them by importance?"

Ava thought for a second. "Of course," she said. At my last job, I worked with many supervisors. They had different needs that our team could fulfill. I compiled a list of all tasks assigned by each supervisor. Then, I shared this list with my leader, and we developed a plan to determine the top priority.

"I also took the time to see if tasks could be completed quickly. I was able to complete half of the list quickly. This process helped save time and money. It was a good practice, and the supervisors were happy with my initiative."

Mr. Hardling sat there with a hard stare. He did not like her and quickly wanted her out of sight. She is doing the most, and why the fuck is she giving all these college-level answers? This shit is not welcome again. Another one that's trying to outdo the shit and look better than me. I won't have this shit again."

Leilani loved this candidate. She could see herself in her, but she was more advanced. "No way was I thinking like this at her age," she thought while reviewing her resume.

She had just graduated from college, and her mindset was strong. She is the best person I have seen all day for this role. I will let Mr. Taylor know that she is the one we should pick. I will cosign for her, no doubt about it.

"Thank you so much, Ava. It was such a pleasure speaking with you today. Do you have any questions for us as this concludes the interview?" Leilani smiled.

"Yes, my first question is, what would a first week look like for this role?"

"Oh my god, are you serious? First question, ugh." Hardling tried to say under his breath, but both Leilani and Ava heard him.

Neither one of them let it faze them, so they both let it roll off their shoulder.

Leilani perked up. "Well, it would start with reading about the past and current projects. I have also created some Excel sheets allowing you to perform basic forecasting. Of course, it has to be kept up to date. She laughed. I have had many long nights with those Excel documents."

Ava looked on very excitedly and stated, "That would be awesome. I love to analyze what is current and how we can make it new."

Hardling stated with a raised tone. "Well, the first week also involves getting to know me and my schedule. It's always best practice for this position to align closely with my day-to-day activities.

"We must finalize everything through Mr. Taylor, as this is his project. Mr. Hardling is well aware of these details." Leilani stated, glaring at Mr. Hardling. "Please continue if you have additional questions."

"Oh well," she looked up at the ceiling. "Does this role prefer an individual to be a self-starter or wait to be provided guidance?"

Leilani spoke up first. "I prefer a person to be about half. There will be times when a task is provided, but there are other times when you should know the next step. If that makes sense, I would always be available for questions and brainstorming."

Harding howled, "I prefer a person to wait and be provided guidance. That way, nothing is being started without my knowledge. This way, we can create a cohesive environment." He started with a perplexed look on his face."

"Any more questions he quickly stated!"

"Just how long will it take for the team to let me know if I got the job?"

"We have a couple more interviews, but we are planning to let everyone know by the end of the week," Mr. Hardling stated aggressively.

Leilani hurriedly jumped in. "He is semi-correct. "You are the last person, so we should make a final decision very soon," she stated with a smile.

Leilani asked Ava if she could stay and chat for a few minutes. She sent Mr. Hardling away because his work for the day was done. His services were no longer needed, she laughed to herself.

**

He walked out of the room, looking like he had smoke coming from his ears while also mugging her.

Leilani sat in the small conference room with Ava, a bright and eager candidate who she believed had made it to the final round. Ava had potential—raw, ambitious, with a quiet confidence that reminded Leilani of herself a year ago.

"You're strong with numbers," Leilani said after the mock assignment. "But I want you to trust your voice in the room, too. Don't just answer—*own* the answer."

Ava nodded, scribbling notes quickly. "I just get nervous that I will sound like I don't know enough or what I'm talking about."

Leilani smiled gently. "Everyone starts there. What matters is how you carry yourself while you grow."

She gave a few more tips, watching Ava absorb every word. She could already see it—the right hire, the right energy.

Then the door swung open.

Hardling.

"Ms. Brooks," he said flatly. "May I speak with you outside for a moment?"

Leilani rose calmly. "Excuse me, Ava. I'll be right back."

Outside the door, Hardling dropped the mask.

"You're overstepping," he snapped. "This isn't your role. Coaching candidates, mentoring them—this isn't your place."

Leilani blinked. "I was asked to lead. Mentorship *is* leadership."

"She's not hired yet," he hissed. "You're acting like she's already yours to mold. This isn't your little personal development project."

Before she could answer, Mr. Taylor's voice cut in from down the hall.

"It *is* her project, Hardling."

They both turned to see Taylor walking toward them, expression unreadable.

"You've made it clear you're uncomfortable with Leilani's elevation," he said, stopping just close enough to keep his voice sharp and clear. "But I'm going to say this once—if I hear about you undermining her again, you'll be finding *your* replacement next."

Mr. Hardling stiffened, face flushed with fury and embarrassment. He ran off to his office, tail tucked between his legs. At that moment, he was defeated.

Mr. Taylor looked at Leilani, saying, "Please continue your session. And when you're done, let's finalize Ava's offer."

Leilani nodded and returned to the room.

When she sat down again, Ava looked up, wide-eyed.

"Is there a problem?"

Leilani smiled, steady and sure. "No, no problem at all. I have great news for you."

*

New Beginnings

The office felt different that morning—charged with quiet change. Ava walked in wearing a soft gray blouse and black slacks, sharp but comfortable. She was early, notebook in hand, nerves steady beneath the surface.

Leilani met her in the lobby.

"Right on time," she said, smiling.

"I didn't sleep last night, still can't believe I got the job," Ava admitted nervously.

"That's normal, it's the same way I felt when I was in your same shoes," Leilani said, touching her shoulder. "Come on. Let's get you settled."

They moved through the halls, a few people glancing at Ava curiously. Leilani ignored them. She gave her a tour, introduced her to the right folks, and explained the unspoken rules of the floor.

"This is your seat now," she said, pausing by the desk that used to be hers. "Your voice belongs in this space."

Ava looked around and then up at Leilani. "You got your vibe going on here, I can tell from the coworkers, you know?"

Leilani smiled, a little sad. "Don't worry about that, before you know it, everyone will be looking for you and your vibe. Give it time."

As they grabbed coffee in the breakroom, Mr. Hardling strolled in with a smile that didn't quite meet his eyes.

"Ms. Tanner," he said to Ava. "I had to make time so I could personally welcome you to my team. We'll discuss later how you can specifically support me, your manager. I will show you how things work around here."

Ava blinked; her face neutral. "I appreciate that, Mr. Hardling. I look forward to learning a lot. Leilani has shown me so much. But Mr. Taylor has been a dream, and he supports me taking after Leilani here." She stated with a smirk.

Leilani sipped her coffee, looking at Mr. Hardling to see his reaction. I like her, but I would have never had the balls to stand up to him, let alone on my first day of work, she thought, laughing to herself.

Hardling nodded stiffly, "Well, Mr. Taylor is a great executive with excellent knowledge and years of experience." He sarcastically said, "We were all so lucky to have him here with us." After that, he hurried and excused himself, then left.

Ava turned to Leilani. "He better stop playing with me. I can be very professionally rude, let's not start this off on the wrong foot."

Leilani laughed. "You are hilarious. He did not know how to take your comment. I have never seen him that flustered. I enjoyed that. Keep it up; he needs that kind of heat so he can back off. He likes to work you hard and take all the credit, so stay on point always."

A few hours later, Leilani finally finished packing the last of her things. Ava returned to the desk after meeting with Mr. Taylor and the other team members. She had learned so much in just one day.

"I hope this isn't the last time we talk. I would love it if you could continue to mentor me and help me progress in my career. I have been waiting on this for so long, and it's finally here. But it's sad cause I'm losing such a great person."

"It won't be, don't even worry about that," Leilani said. "We're in each other's corner now. I will always be there for you. Maybe this weekend we can catch up, I have a date with my cousin Maeve. You will love her, she is such a good time."

They hugged, one long and grounding hug as if they had known each other for years.

When Leilani walked out that door for the last time, she didn't look back. She was eager for her new role and the new journey ahead. She's now thrilled to have a new friend in her corner, which is unusual because she doesn't typically trust people.

She didn't need to because she had Marquise, and she believed that was all she needed at the time.

Now she was ready to go home. She hopped into her Nissan Ultima, her mind filled with a multitude of thoughts.

"What you didn't know I bossed up and got a new ride. Now that I'm not taking care of Goofy, I can move a lot better. Yeah, it's a used vehicle, but I got a good deal, mind ya business. Damn, I can't tell yall everything. Keep up with me on my journey."

Leilani had a good day preparing Ava for her new role. Leilani knows Ava will do great because she will ensure she's with her every step of the way, always and forever. She is stuck with me, and I see a lot of my younger self in Ava. She is just more advanced than I am.

No more Marquise, she thought she was excited to be meeting with chemistry soon, I have so much to look forward to. She pulled off smiling.

Later that night, Leilani sat on her back porch, which was enclosed with privacy tape on the windows. Leilani was wrapped in her favorite silky robe, a glass of mixed liquor in one hand, her journal open in the other. The city lights blinked below, familiar and far away all at once.

She stared at the last page she'd written weeks ago—right before the rooftop, the internship, and everything.

Back then, she had scribbled questions:

What if I'm not enough? What if I made a mistake leaving? What if he was right about me?

She read the questions slowly, then grabbed her pen and drew a thick line beneath them.

And then, in bold handwriting, wrote:

I was always enough. I just stopped asking for permission. There was no mistake made when leaving. I am stronger and wiser now, and there is no way he was right about me. I have a new person who is interested in me, and he has never asked me for money. I'm moving on and up!

She looked out at the skyline and let herself feel it—the grief of who she used to be, the joy of who she was becoming. Her career was rising. Her boundaries were firm. Her heart, for once, felt like her own.

She didn't need the world to clap.

She didn't need Marquise to regret it, Hardling to respect it, or anyone else to validate the life she was building.

She just needed to keep showing up.

And she would.

Because she was her proof now, and the only way to go was up from here.

**

Leilani went back into her house to sit while the TV played a show in the background. She was not watching the show, but the show was watching her, when a soft knock pulled her from her thoughts. Leilani stood, surprised, and peeked through the door. Chemistry stood there, hoodie on, two carry-out containers in his hands.

"Didn't know if you ate," he said, holding up the containers. "Thought I'd check on you."

She smiled and let him in. "You always show up when I need someone."

They sat on the floor this time, food spread out between them, her back door open so they could feel the breeze. The comfort was easy, the air was fresh, and his presence made it even easier.

He watched her closely. "You've had a hell of a season."

She nodded. "Feels like I've been running uphill for months."

"But you didn't stop," he said. "Even when you were scared. Even when they tried to box you in, you pushed through."

She looked down, overwhelmed by his sincerity. "I don't even know who I'm becoming half the time."

"I do," he said, his voice low and warm. "You're becoming the woman you were always meant to be. The one who doesn't ask for space—she *takes* it. The one who inspires other people just by walking in her truth."

She blinked fast, not wanting to cry. "Why do you always know what to say? You always have to uplift me without even trying. You're always encouraging me for no reason."

He leaned in a little, his eyes never leaving hers. "Because I'm falling for you, Leilani. Hard. It's also not hard to be there and uplift such a beautiful person. You have encouraged me, and I just met you. No one can look at me and see potential; I don't know how to feel myself."

She didn't move away.

Didn't flinch.

She just whispered, "You got me falling for you, too. But I'm scared, I don't want to be used again. I don't want to ruin what we have so far."

And this time, she let herself feel his love, her strength, and their moment.

For once, she wasn't afraid of being loved right.

She was ready for it, even though she was a little scared at the moment. But that was fine; she was prepared to leap; she would no longer hold back.

With that, she kissed Chemistry so profoundly that it took her breath away. She pulled her face away and smiled so hard that her cheeks hurt.

He just looked at her with so much admiration and love, thinking to himself, "Is this really what he wants?" No one has ever made him feel like this. He notices he is also a bit nervous. He does not want his life to push her away. There's so much that she doesn't know about him. However, he controls his life; no one will take his little smart baby from him.

*

Growth Together – A New Rhythm

The weeks that followed unfolded like the slow bloom of something real. They weren't rushing. There were no grand declarations, no labels thrown around too soon. But everything between Leilani and Chemistry began to settle into a rhythm—easy, grounded, and undeniable.

They sent each other good morning texts that turned into midday check-ins. Shared playlists. Shared books. On Sundays, he'd meet her after the farmer's market and carry her bags like it was nothing.

She turned to him on one of those Sundays while they sat on a park bench under a warm sky. "You know," she said, "I am enjoying spending time with you doing different activities. It does not feel like a distraction, more like a connection. I'm just worried that things will change; it feels too good to be true."

Chemistry looked over at her, smiling slowly and sincerely. "I'm glad you feel our connection because that's all I feel when I'm with you. I feel like you and me it's in alignment with the universe. Please don't worry, nothing will change unless you or I make a change. I'm with you, my little smart baby."

She let that sit as so many thoughts crossed her mind. However, she argued with herself, saying, "He is not Marquise; he will not use me. Who cares if he's saying all the right things, like Marquise? He is NOT fucking Marquise. I deserve to be happy."

He wasn't trying to fix her. He wasn't trying to control her. He just showed up, every day, like love didn't have to be complicated to be real.

And Leilani let herself lean into it for the first time in a long time.

Into him.

Into something steady, tender, and unshakable.

They weren't just building; they were trying to make it last.

Leilani moved closer and placed her lips on his, their lips connecting in a kiss. She was enjoying him so much, and he was right—I don't need to worry. Currently, it's going great. Once that changes, then I will worry, she thought.

**

Later that day, Leilani woke up to the sound of her phone vibrating again, the screen flashing in the darkness of her bedroom.

Why is Marquise calling me this late?? He is getting on my nerves. I had a good day, and I don't need this shit.

She groaned, rubbing her eyes before flipping the phone over.

Missed Calls: 15.

Voicemails: 7.

Text Messages: 23.

He needs to get a life. Where is his wife? Is she not keeping tabs on him? Ugh. Her stomach twisted. She knew ignoring him would set him off, but she hadn't expected this level of persistence. She scrolled through the texts, each one worse than the last:

"You really gon do me like this?"

"After everything I did for you?"

"I know where you live. You forget that?"

"Don't make me come find you."

She sat up straight at that one, her pulse spiking.

Then another text popped up.

"Open the door."

Leilani froze. Her breath caught in her throat, her fingers tightening around the phone. **No. He wouldn't. He's bluffing.**

BANG. BANG. BANG.

She jumped. **Oh, shit.**

The knocks were heavy, urgent.

"Leilani, open up the damn door!" Marquise's voice was sharp, laced with anger.

Her heart pounded as she swung her legs over the side of the bed. She wasn't ready for this. She wasn't prepared to face him. But I guess now is the best time for it.

She tiptoed toward the window, peeking out. His car was parked outside, his silhouette dark against the porch light.

Another bang on the door.

"Yo, for real? You ghostin' me now? After all we've been through?" His voice dropped lower, almost pleading. "C'mon, baby. Just let me talk to you."

Her stomach churned. The **gaslighting** was starting already.

She forced herself to take a breath. **Think. Stay calm.**

"Marquise get cho ass from in front of my door. Where is your wife at you need to be checking for her and get the fuck off my steps. Don't nobody care you came over here I'm not opening my damn door and I'm not fucking with you. How the fuck you find out where I live anyway, you're a stalker."

"I'm not going no fucking where you gone talk to me. And don't worry about my wife she where she needs to be not in my fucking business. You're damn right I'm a stalker. What did you think? You were going to move on without me? You are mines; I don't care about all that moving on shit you belong to me. I'm all you got, nobody else will want you like me, they're just going to use you." Marquise stated!

She swallowed hard, holding onto her phone. She was about to cuss his ass clean out again but she got another vibration. She signed loudly, thinking it was from Marquise. But no, it was her baby texting, as if he knew what was happening.

Chemistry: What's up, my smart baby? You good over there? How *are you feeling?*

Her breath caught. **How did he know?**

She hesitated and then hurried up and called him.

"Damn it's like you knew was is going on. Stated Leilani."

"What? What is going on over there?" Ask Chemistry.

She answered quietly. "Marquise is over here banging on my door trying to get me to open up. I don't even know how he found out where I live."

"Alright, keep that door locked until I get there." His voice was sharp, alert.

**

"Wait, once you –" she yelled without thinking.
Click.

He hung up.

Leilani's hands were shaking now, her mind racing. She turned back toward the door. The knocking had stopped, but she knew Marquise was still out there.

Minutes passed.

Then, headlights cut through the window.

A car door slammed.

And then—another voice.

"You need to get the fuck outa here. The fuck you on anyway coming to someone house uninvited. This is a whole female who is living alone, and you are trying to scare her while she is in her safe environment."

She thought that he was so strong and caring in chemistry.

Leilani's heart thumped into her chest. What am I feeling about this man? I haven't known him for long.

Marquise's voice dropped, but she could hear the tension through the door. "Who the fuck are you? And why are you here at my girl's house? We are going through a tough time right now and don't need any extras in the mix."

"It doesn't matter what you over here tryna do play boy, she good, she done with you. You gon step off this porch, or we gon have a different type of conversation."

A tense silence followed.

Then Marquise laughed. "Man, you got her feeling herself, huh? Got her thinking she's somebody now?" His voice turned mean. "She ain't nobody, bruh. She's just a chick who loves to play house, but she ain't built for the real thing. That's why I had to have **options. Which she knew about the whole time.**"

Leilani clenched her fists.

"That's why you're at her door like a whole clown? Is that why you are at her doorstep, begging to be let into a house you don't pay bills for? Player if she wanted you in this motherfucker, you would have a key." Chemistry shot back, his voice calm but sharp. "You done here so you need to move the fuck around for you get ya ass beat."

Another pause. Then Marquise's footsteps.

Leilani held her breath, listening as he walked off the porch.

Then his voice, just before getting into his car:

"This ain't over yet, I will get my woman back." He yelled

The tires screeched as he pulled off, leaving silence in his wake.

Leilani exhaled, her hands gripping the phone as if it were a lifeline.

Then—knock, knock.

Soft. Not urgent.

"Leilani," Chemistry called through the door. "You can open up. He's gone."

She hesitated, then unlocked the door, opening it just enough to see his face.

He looked her over, checking. "You good?"

Leilani swallowed the lump in her throat and ran up to chemistry, hugging him. "Man, his lame ass won't leave me alone. I don't want him anymore, I don't know how many times I have to say this shit."

"You will be okay you got me and no fuck boy will get in the way of that," he said hugging her back tightly. "C'mon. Let's get out of here for a bit." Grabbing her hand, he led her to his ride.

She stared at him, at the way he took control not in a possessive manner but protective, solid, **honest—** and she knew.

Everything just changed!

She allowed him to grab her hand and followed him to the car. He opened the door for her. She kissed him and slid into the passenger side of the vehicle.

Leilani sat in Chemistry's car, her hands still shaking in her lap. The city lights blurred through the windshield as he drove, silently giving her the space she needed. She could still hear Marquise's voice in her head, mocking and dismissing her like she was nothing.

"Man, you got her feeling herself, huh? Got her thinking she's somebody now?" His voice turned mean. "She ain't nobody, bruh. Leilani mocked.

Her stomach turned. She had spent years being his provider, emotional cushion, and safe place. And to hear him say those words like she was dumb? Like she had to stay with him, as if he were the only man in this world.

Yes, I am that girl on the bus who is scared to be left alone. I am scared that no one will be waiting for me when I get home, making me feel like I don't have anyone at home who loves me.

"Stop it right now, Lei. He is not the only one who wants you. I want you; that's a hurt man who lost a good woman. He is upset that you don't want to have anything to do with him. He's pathetic, that's all he's done, lost his angel, but I'm right here to claim the bright light," he stated while smiling."

She looked over at him, cheesing. She was smiling so hard it was contagious, and she loosened her grip. He wasn't wrong about me.

They drove in silence for a few more blocks before he spoke again.

"You wanna talk about it? Of course, we don't have to if you're uncomfortable with it. I'm not trying to pressure you on this. I want you to know that I am always here for you. You can't get rid of me now," he looked at her and smiled with those beautiful teeth.

Leilani stared out the window, her mind replaying everything. Marquise was standing at her door. The pounding. The threats. The way he laughed, like he still had power over her. And then chemistry showed up, steady and unshaken.

"I don't even know where to start," she admitted. "I feel like he is not worth my time, and I want nothing more to do with him. I am tired of telling him the same thing."

"You don't owe me anything. You take all the time you need." He tapped his fingers on the steering wheel. Whenever you are ready, say whatever comes first."

She hesitated, but then the words tumbled out. "I feel stupid after all these years of being with that man."

"For what?"

"For... everything." She rubbed her temples. "For believing him. For letting him use me. For thinking he loved me." She swallowed. "And for believing he was sorry for how he treated me. When he got the chance, he could not wait to tell me how he felt about me."

Chemistry shook his head. "That ain't stupid. That's human. You were with that lame for years. You were doing what you have always done, you did not know any better."

She let that sit for a moment, breathing through the knot in her chest.

"What if he doesn't leave me alone? What the fuck I'm supposed to do I don't call the fucking police and I can't fight a man" she stated angrily.

"He won't. Not right away. He does not want his angel to get away." Chemistry's tone was even, but there was an edge beneath it. "Men like him? They don't like losin' what they think they own."

Leilani flinched.

"But you ain't his anymore, I want you," Chemistry continued, glancing at her. "And he's going to learn that quickly. Or I will take his ass to school and offer him a lesson he won't forget."

She exhaled, feeling a strange mix of anger and relief. Angry because Marquise wasn't done and wouldn't leave her be, she felt relief because maybe she was done and ready to move on with the handsome man sitting next to her.

Chemistry pulled into a small 24-hour diner. "C'mon," he said. "You need food."

"I don't think I can eat."

"You gon sit in there with me and at least try," he said, already opening his door. "Cuz you still shaking, and I don't like that shit." He said, walking around to help her out of the car.

She looked at him for a moment, then nodded.

And for the first time in a long time, she let someone take care of her. Again, she looked into his eyes, memorized, and gave him another long, deep kiss. He was making her happy, and he had only been here briefly.

*

Marquise's Next Move

Marquise sat in his car, his hands gripping the steering wheel so tightly that his knuckles turned white. The city lights cast shadows over his face, making the anger in his eyes look darker.

This wasn't supposed to happen.

Leilani was supposed to **break**, not disappear. She was supposed to **crawl back**, not move the hell on. And who the fuck was that dude?

He took a slow breath, forcing himself to think. He had let his temper get the best of him tonight, pulling up on her like that. He should have been smoother and more patient. But seeing her with another man? Laughing, talking, looking **free?**

That shit burned. And he needed to figure out if he could smooth it over. The main thing was to see how close her and this nigga got. Cause I don't work that hard, but for Leilani, I don't know if I could let her go.

He grabbed his phone, scrolling through his contacts until he found the name he was looking for.

Monica (Wife).

He smirked to himself before hitting the call button.

She answered on the second ring. "Hey, baby," she said, all sweet and oblivious. "You coming home? I got some scenes for us to do on Instagram. We're on a roll and want to keep the momentum going. We have been gaining more followers since we went on that cruise. This shit is lit, our bag is going to be lovely for this month."

"Yeah," he said smoothly, leaning back in his seat. "Just wanted to hear your voice first. You know I'm all about making more money. Shit we always on money moves. This has been our best plan yet."

He lied, he was tired, and wanted a woman who tried to build honestly, like Leilani. My wife and I have been like this for years. They have been looking for get-rich-quick schemes to make money as a married couple. We have dealt with false reporting, her passing out while I was lifting things of high value, and even some embezzlement. This social media shit has been the best lick for us lately.

That's why he has not been asking Leilani for any money. He believed he had changed, but she overlooked his glow-up. She's so busy in this new nigga face, but they both don't see me coming, he thought!

His wife, giggling, snatched him from his thoughts. "Awww, you're so cute. I was just about to post the pictures from our lunch the other day with the kids— our likes and comments are still going up from the cruise ones!"
He smiled, but it didn't reach his eyes. "Yeah, you do that, babe. Let 'em know we're solid. Show them what truly locked in looks like!"

Because that's what people like Monica cared about—appearances. Attention. And she was so caught up in it, she'd never see what was happening right in front of her. She didn't understand that her husband was changing. He wanted privacy and happiness, not living up to anyone's expectations.

His fingers drummed against the leather armrest.

Leilani thought she was done with him. She figured she could disappear without a word. Meet a new nigga, like she's about to live happily ever after. And yeah, she's right. I followed her after work to find out where she lives. Imagine my surprise to find out that she lives in a house; she's doing it like that.

What did she forget that I knew where she worked? However, it was weird that she was carrying boxes and other items out last Friday, as if she had been fired.

She left me no choice, and she didn't give me one word after she left our apartment. I gave her time to calm down and understand our new world. She had the time needed to be okay with what we are doing as a team. I don't see how this has changed anything. She can continue to do her and be with me. I have my own money now and can take care of her.

But Nah.

She wasn't getting off that easily, though. Not if I have anything to do with it. She's going to see and love this glow up I've got going on now.

When he had unfinished business. And here she is smiling and entertaining some new nigga like he never fucking existed.

I'm not giving up without a fight, and I can promise that!

Marquise steps through the front door, exhausted from the long day, but his mind is elsewhere. He barely notices his kids running up to him, their voices a mix of excitement and playful teasing. His youngest, a five-year-old boy, jumps into his arms, while his ten-year-old daughter gives him a shy hug before retreating to the dinner table. He also had a six-month-old, but he figured she was asleep. He followed them to the kitchen.

"Hey, champ," Marquise says, his voice warm but distracted, as he holds his son. He kisses his daughter's head before letting her go.

"How was your day, daddy?" his daughter asks, trying to get his attention.

"Same as usual," he replies with a forced smile, setting his son down before looking around the kitchen. His wife, Monica, is already busy at the stove, humming softly, but her eyes are fixed on her phone. The camera flashes from Instagram are almost constant as she snaps pictures of their meal.

Marquise sits down at the table, pulling his chair out deliberately slowly. His eyes momentarily flick toward Monica. She doesn't look up from her phone, her fingers scrolling and tapping with practiced ease.

"Dinner smells amazing, babe," he says, trying to inject a little warmth into his voice. Monica doesn't look up, but she smiles in acknowledgment.

"Thank you," she murmurs, still focused on getting the perfect shot for her latest post.

The kids start digging into their food, and Marquise follows suit. His movements are methodical, but his mind drifts to Leilani. He pushes the thought away and forces himself to engage with his family, even as his obsession with her bubbles under the surface.

"Mom, can I have some juice?" his daughter asks, and Monica slides a glass toward her without breaking her rhythm.

"Sure, sweetie. But make sure you're smiling for the camera, okay?" Monica adds, snapping another picture of the meal, which features the kids.

Marquise's jaw tightens slightly. Monica is always on her phone, posting, sharing, and curating an image of their perfect family. But as he watches her, his thoughts slide back to Leilani, that raw, unrelenting anger and yearning to have her in his life again.

"Monica, where is the baby? Are you bringing her down here with us?"

"Naw, I just put her down. Please don't wake her up. It's so much work dealing with a newborn," she said, never looking up from her phone. "But hey, at least they are eating up her pictures. I'm not surprised, though, she looks just like her momma."

Marquise looked at her with a look of disgust. He said nothing else; he would see his baby after dinner.

Despite everything, he was very excited about his new baby. He loved children, which is his weakness.

After dinner, Monica scrolls through her phone, typing a caption for her latest post, as the kids run off to watch TV. Marquise stands, clearing all the plates with mechanical precision, his eyes narrowing as he moves around the kitchen. He's suddenly energized, his thoughts clicking into place.

He pauses at the counter, staring at his reflection in the window above the sink. He rubs his hand over his chin, deep in thought. The plan needs to be perfect, something subtle but decisive. His obsession with Leilani has never really gone away, and now, after the way she'd shut him out... he couldn't let it end like that. Not when she was so close to him, so vulnerable, so... perfect.

Marquise ran upstairs to see his baby girl. Entering the room, he was drawn to the baby's scent. He looked at his daughter sleeping peacefully in a bassinet.

Her room was all soft powder pink. He set everything up, from the bassinet to the changing table and the rugs. He wanted nothing but the best for his children. What's crazy is that Leilani made some of this happen. She is such a big part of my life, he thought. His thoughts made him sad because he had never considered getting Leilani pregnant, but he bet she would be a fantastic mother.

"Aww, you're all so cute, and I snapped a couple of pictures without you noticing. I know these will bust for the gram." Monica stated, pulling him from his thoughts.

"Damn Monica," Marquise whispered. You said I couldn't wake her up, and here you come, disturbing the peace."

"It was just a cute moment, Marquise. It would be good for the algorithm, plus, they love pictures of baby Kiara." She smiled, walking off and back downstairs.

Damn she gets on my damn nerves he thought. He looked over at his baby girl still sleep unaware of the fuckery her mother be on. He leaned down, kissed her soft cheek, and smiled as he admired his daughter. He checked to ensure the baby monitor was functional, and then he walked out of the room backwards, making sure not to make a sound.

He ran downstairs, feeling more at peace, which is how he always felt around his children." Monica," he called, turning to his wife, who didn't look up from her phone.

"Hmm?" she hums absentmindedly.

He hesitates for a moment before speaking, the words tasting bitter. "I'm gonna go out briefly, clear my head."

Monica's eyes flick up briefly, but only to make sure her phone's flash is aligned. "Okay. Just don't be too long. I have to get some posts ready for tomorrow."

Marquise nods, his eyes lingering on her, feeling the disconnection between them. He walks to the door, his thoughts far away from his family, far from Monica's relentless pursuit of online perfection.

Outside, under the dim streetlight, he lets out a breath. The plan begins to form. He could manipulate Leilani—pull her back with charm, maybe find something to hold over Chemistry. That would do it. He could show her the life he could give her, the life she'd never have with anyone else.

Or maybe… he thought, tapping his foot against the ground, his hands balled into fists. He could dig deeper and find something about chemistry that could ruin him. Get close to him. Find his weaknesses. After all, Chemistry had something Marquise wanted—Leilani.

He couldn't let her slip away. No. He was *obsessed* and would have her back, no matter what it took.

*

Later the next day, he found himself driving in his car. The sun was still low, casting a soft orange glow over the city. He had told Monica he was working late and needed to clear his head, but his mind was consumed with the thought of Leilani.

He'd already spent the night pacing, unable to sleep, and had woken with a singular, obsessive thought: *He couldn't let her escape. Not now, not ever.*

Now, he found himself following Leilani as if she were going somewhere. He needed information on her life to weasel his way back in. He did not want her to meet up with that character.

His fingers gripped the steering wheel so tightly his knuckles were white, but he refused to let his mind wander. His eyes stayed focused ahead as he drove. He kept hidden, his car blending with the early morning traffic.

He parked a few blocks from the park, watching the scene through his car's tinted windows. The park was quiet, almost serene, and the sun's rays filtered through the trees.

He spotted Leilani almost immediately—her bright smile, the way she moved with that effortless grace. But it wasn't just her that caught his attention. That character stood with her now—that smug, self-satisfied bastard.

Marquise could feel his blood pressure rising as the two chuckled. He was leaning in too close, his hand brushing against Leilani's arm in a way that made Marquise's stomach turn.

He watched them from the safety of his car, his breath coming in shallow gasps. *How could she be so damn casual with him?* It angered him that they seemed to have some strong bond—a connection he could never seem to replicate with Leilani. But he *would* get her back.

Minutes dragged on, stretching into what felt like hours. He wanted to storm over there, confront them, but he knew better. He needed to be patient. He needed to gather information. He had to know who this person was and identify their weaknesses. There had to be something he could use to his advantage.

Eventually, the dude said something to Leilani that made her laugh again. Her head tilted back, that beautiful sound ringing in his ears. His nostrils flared, and his palms started to sweat in his lap, but he stayed still, waiting.

When they finally stood to leave, Marquise kept his distance, his eyes never leaving them. He wrapped his arms around her hips as she hugged his neck. She placed a nice soft kiss on his lips. Marquise was livid, and it took everything in him not to storm over to both of them.

They parted ways, with Leilani going one way and chemistry going another. Marquise decided to follow him from a safe distance, careful not to be noticed.

He followed him as he walked through a busy neighborhood, keeping a few steps behind. The adrenaline buzzed in his veins. He was worried because he was not from this neighborhood and didn't want to draw too much attention.

He stopped in front of a small, old house with a white picket fence. The door to the house opened. A woman, with long braids reaching her ass and dressed in a tight black and white one-piece body suit, stepped out. The typical rat ass bitch he thought to himself.

She greeted him with an easy, open hug and kiss on both cheeks. Marquise's stomach churned. He could hear her laughter from where he stood, faint but enough to fuel the fire of jealousy and rage building inside him.

Marquise's eyes narrowed. *Who the hell was she?* He watched Chemistry wrap an arm around her waist, leading her back into the house, their laughter and voices blending in a sickening symphony.

He stayed there, frozen momentarily, his anger pushing down on him. He'd find the cracks in ol' boy's perfect life and see what he could use against him. Starting with who this woman is.

And once he had them, *Leilani would be his again.*

He looked at the house, the shadows creeping across the lawn as the door shut behind them, sealing the possibility of getting his woman back.

Marquise exhaled sharply, the bitterness settling in his throat. He turned and returned to his car, his mind already spinning with the possibilities. He was done being patient. He had a plan. And the next time he saw Leilani, it would be on *his* terms.

*

Leilani's First Week

Leilani smoothed her hands down the front of her blazer as she stood outside the sleek office building. The morning sun reflected off the tall glass windows, and she felt like she was walking into something meant for her for the first time in a long time.

Not something she was doing for someone else.

Her stomach flipped with nerves, but she took a deep breath and stepped inside.

The lobby was bustling—professionals in tailored suits walked past her, their voices blending into a hum of ambition.

She stood there in the lobby with her thoughts getting the best of her. All of a sudden, her clothes didn't feel professional enough, the voices grew louder, so loud she almost couldn't stand, and her breathing started to become shallow. She felt like a seashell in an ocean of professional seekers.

"What if I fail? What if they realize I don't know enough? What if—"

"You got this."

She heard Chemistry's voice in her head, steady and sure, as he had said it last night before she finally fell asleep. She had woken up to a simple text from him this morning:

"Day 1. Show 'em why they picked you."

A small smile touched her lips as she straightened her posture and approached the front desk. "Hi, I'm Leilani. I'm here for my first day as an intern with the project management team."

The receptionist smiled. "Welcome! You'll be with Ms. Carter—she's expecting you."

Leilani nodded, following her through the glass doors and down a hallway lined with offices. The space was open, modern, **efficient**—everything she had dreamed of being a part of.

"This is where I'm supposed to be," she told herself.

Inside a bright corner office, a woman in her late forties stood up from her desk. Her fitted navy dress and natural curls gave her effortless confidence.

"Hi Leilani, it's great to have you finally," she said, extending a hand. "As you know, I'm Simone Carter. I was almost getting nervous that Mr. Taylor would not release you."

Leilani shook her hand. "Thank you so much for this opportunity."

Simone smiled. "Oh, trust me, I was excited to meet you. I don't take interns unless I see something in them. And from what I've read and heard, you've got real potential."

Leilani felt her chest tighten. She wasn't used to hearing that. **Potential.** As if she were someone who could become **something.**

"Come on," Simone continued, grabbing a tablet. "I'll introduce you to the team and get you settled in."

Leilani followed her, still nervous but with something new beneath it.

Hope. She has found a new place in this world, she thought, smiling.

Simone took her around and introduced her to her peers in the office. There were five other project managers: Elio, Zephyr, Ozias, Iris, and Allegra. They all had office spaces similar to Simone's. This team of project managers had different areas of focus. Some handled city contracts, special events, and government events, among others.

"Don't worry about remembering what everyone does. For now, please focus on my area, which, as you know, is city contracts. That's your bread and butter for right now. So, we will start with what you know and see how it goes from there." Simone smiled at Leilani.

"That sounds so amazing," stated Leilani. "I'm so excited to jump right in. Ready to start digging into the various current projects."

"See, it's that enthusiasm that I enjoy about you. This is why I am a bit nervous about losing you too soon." She laughed, "You're so fast at learning from what I have heard. She looked over at Leilani and winked.

She walked Leilani over to the cubicles where all the interns were seated. She was the fourth person to arrive. She introduced Leilani and asked her to review the package on her desktop to catch up on her current projects.

Simone explained that at least four interns are on site each season. She just happened to get the last spot, so she was lucky number four. There were two men named Aurelius and Caius, and another woman named Lorelei.

Lorelei already showed that we were in some concealed competition. Women like her crack me up, and they're always funny to me. I'm better off as your friend than your comp. I only compete with myself because my opinion is the only opinion that matters.

Aurelius was a pretty cool, chilled, and laid-back person. He is the nicest one out of the bunch. He immediately clears up any confusion, just like a big brother. He seems protective, and we've only just met today.

Now, Caius, my man, just would not shut up. He has been over-talking everyone since I sat down. Since he likes talking, I will use him to get most of the information. "So, Caius, which project manager do you belong to?" Leilani asked.

"There is no belonging; it depends on your work ethic around here," he said. "I have been here the longest, a little over two years. I have worked with all six project managers; they consider me an asset to the company." He boasted.

"Yes, we all experience every area because we work with all managers." Said Aurelius, "If you're good enough, you can transfer to a better job within the company." He said, cutting his eyes over to Caius.

Before Caius could make a slick comment, Zephyr came walking up. "Hey guys, mind if I borrow Caius for a second?"

"Yes," we all said in unison. Caius got up and walked off with Zephyr with a satisfying smirk. My fake big brother spoke up when they were out of earshot.

"Don't mind him, Leilani, he's full of himself. It's normal for him to think he means more to his supervisor than any other intern. I mean if he was why the fuck has his job title not changed yet." Aurelius said, laughing.

"He is pretty good, though; he knows the managers' processes and personality. If you ask me, we could all learn from him because he has been here longer than us." Lorelei stated.

Aurelius looked over at Leilani and mouth silently "She is an ass kisser". Leilani put a small smile on her face. Thinking well, I guess I got her number and need to stay out of the way; she seems like a snitch.

"Well, don't worry, Leilani. If you need anything, please ask me, " Aurelius said.

"Thank you, Aurelius. I appreciate that." Leilani unlocked her computer and opened the package Simone wanted her to analyze.

She had been reviewing the current projects for over an hour. She was so excited that she could not wait to dig in. This was the best part for her: checking all the projects and ensuring nothing was missed. I am going to love this job, she thought, smiling. She would continue reading until the end of her day.

Later that afternoon, Leilani continued to sit at the desk, analyzing the data sent from Simone. She was settling into her shared desk space and reviewing a project timeline. She was already sending ideas and comments on current projects.

After a few moments, she felt her phone vibrate.

A text from **Simone.**

"Nice job today. I can tell you're going to do well here. I have already been hearing great things."

Leilani exhaled, a slow, steady release of pressure she didn't even realize she was holding.

She had made it through the first day.

Not only had she survived, but she also felt like she had contributed.

For the first time in a long time, she felt... proud of her current job.

*

Her fingers hovered over her phone.

For years, whenever something big happened, her first instinct had been to call Marquise. To share her wins, hoping he'd be proud, too.

But now?

Her mind went somewhere else.

Before she could overthink it, she scrolled to **Chemistry's** name, typed a message, and hit send.

"I got through Day 1. My boss said she sees real potential in me."

His reply came almost instantly.

"What did I tell you? Ain't no surprise. You the truth. That deserves a real celebration."

Leilani smiled, shaking her head.

She didn't even argue this time.

Maybe... she did deserve to celebrate.

And maybe... it would be good to let someone new be proud of her. He seems genuine, and she could feel it through his actions.

By Wednesday, she had streamlined an outdated project schedule, catching errors no one else had noticed. This was gaining her more attention from the interns and other project managers.

Monday and Tuesday were dedicated to her learning the company's culture. She also used this time to learn about **current projects from all the project managers.**

On Wednesday, Leilani made it her duty to get to know the workers around the building, not just the interns or the project manager. She wanted the front desk and cleaning staff to get to know her. Leilani was excited to be in a new job and a friendly environment.

On Thursday, Simone **asked her opinion in a strategy meeting, which she requested.** She couldn't believe Simone already trusted her feedback on strategy meetings.

By Friday afternoon, Leilani was exhausted—but it was the *best* kind of exhaustion.

The kind that came from **progress.**

The week had been a whirlwind—learning the systems, sitting in on meetings, taking notes like her life depended on it. Simone had thrown her into real work from day one, and instead of sinking, she had found herself swimming.

Fast. This environment is significantly better than my previous job. My ideas really matter here. No matter what the other interns say. I'm ready to take all this shit over.

Today, she *wrapped up a report on a tight deadline, and Simone gave her the kind of nod that said, "Yeah, you're doing something right."*

Leilani shut down her computer and leaned back in her chair, exhaling.

She had spent so much of her life **proving her worth to people who never saw it.** Now, for the first time, she was proving it to *herself.*

Her phone buzzed.

Chemistry: *Damn, I was starting to think you forgotten about me.*

She smirked, texting back.

Leilani: *I've been busy; it's been a long week.*

Chemistry: *I know. That's why we're celebrating this weekend—my treat. You pick the place.*

She hesitated for a moment, but then... why not? For once, she had something to celebrate.

Leilani: Yes, that sounds like fun. *It's Saturday night. I'll let you know where.*

Chemistry: *That's what I like to hear. See ya soon.*

Leilani put her phone down, grabbed her bag, and headed for the elevator.

She was finally in control of her life for the first time in years.

Leilani was grateful for the end of her first week at the new job, but exhaustion weighed heavily on her. The long hours of navigating new systems, meeting new people, and learning fresh expectations had taken their toll. She was ready to leave the office behind, if only for a few hours.

The bright glow of the office's fluorescent lights seemed to dim as she grabbed her purse, checking the time. It was nearly 6:30 PM, and she could already hear the laughter and chatter of the office's Friday mood. She quickly slipped her jacket on and headed out of the building.

"See you next week, Leilani. I hope you have a great weekend. You did great this week; keep it up, "said Aurelius.

"Thanks, Brother. I will see you next week, and I hope you also have a good weekend." Leilani waved goodbye. The other two were already gone for the day, which is good; she did not want to acknowledge them anyway.

And this weekend?

She was going to enjoy it. But first, she would link up with her cousin and Ava from her old job.

*

Leilani's First Friday

Her cousin **Maeve** had called earlier that afternoon, encouraging Leilani to join her for a drink. "It's your first Friday, Leilani! You *need* to get out and unwind, and you never have fun! Plus, you got rid of that lame, there's no other perfect time for the turn up."

Ava, a friendly face from her previous job, had texted her, asking what she was up to for the weekend. She would love to catch her up on everything that has been going on in the office since she left. Leilani had liked Ava's down-to-earth nature since the first day they met, and seeing a familiar face after a long week of meeting new people would be a welcome break.

The night was incredible, the sky a mix of soft purples and pinks as she walked up to the bar. She met Maeve outside, her cousin grinning widely as she hugged her.

"You made it! I was starting to think you would chicken out," Maeve teased. She was dressed in a skin-tight catsuit. It was blue with a white strip running down the side. She felt cute moving her slim body left and right, her dark lace frontal was bone straight reaching the top of her ass and it was styled effortlessly.

Leilani laughed, shrugging. "I needed a good reason to leave the office. I might be exhausted, but I can't miss this." Leilani wore a tight-fitting green dress that stopped just above her knees, showcasing her toned body and legs. She wore cute black Timberland boots with diamond earrings to complete the look. She had things. She was rarely invited to go outside and party; she was always stuck under Marquise.

They went inside, where the low hum of conversation and the clink of glasses filled the space. When she saw them, Ava was already sitting at a table near the back, waving at them.

"Leilani! Over here!" Ava greeted with a wide smile. She was dressed in a simple but elegant black dress, her hair perfectly pinned up. Ava had a quiet confidence about her that Leilani admired.

"Ava, hi babe, nice to see you," said Leilani, giving her a small hug. "Maeve, this is my new bestie, Ava. She is such a sweet girl."

"Nice to meet you, Ava!" Stated Maeve.

"Awww, Leilani is so sweet, and it's nice to meet you, Maeve."

After ordering their drinks, the three women settled into conversation, the warmth of the bar slowly melting away the stress of the week. Maeve, who has always been the life of the party, regaled them with stories from the hood, while Ava shared tidbits of her own life, updating Leilani on all the mess Mr. Hardling has been on since she left.

"So, how's your first week been, Leilani?" Ava asked, sipping her cocktail.

Leilani smiled, setting her drink down. "Honestly? It's been a lot. I'm still figuring things out, but

I'm getting there. It's been so exciting, though I work with six project managers. I am working with Simone right now, but my learning is super-fast."

"Yeah, the first few weeks are always the hardest," Maeve said, winking at her. "But you'll hit your stride. You've got this. Plus, you're so smart, I'm not worried about you and that work. You will kill it soon enough."

Leilani nodded, feeling the weight of her cousin's reassurance. Her support matters more than she knows; her cousin makes her feel so loved. She didn't realize how much she needed this moment until now—the laughter, the familiarity, the sense of belonging.

They laughed, shared stories, and unwound together as the night continued. Leilani could feel the walls of her stress slowly crumbling. It wasn't just the drinks or the music but the people—the connection. It was nice, for the first time in a long while, to just let go.

The laughter between Leilani, Maeve, and Ava carried on, the clink of their glasses almost musical as they joked about their week. Leilani had just finished telling a funny story from her first day at the new job when a voice broke through the haze of good-natured chatter.

******

"Well, well, if it isn't Leilani."

Leilani froze mid-sentence, her heart rate kicking up. She turned toward the voice. Standing by the bar, with a half-empty glass of whiskey in his hand, was Marquise. His broad shoulders and dark, expensive jacket stood out in the low light of the bar. He wasn't alone either—a guy was with him, nodding in Leilani's direction.

Maeve caught Leilani's look. She quickly got on her bullshit because he was not about to upset my cousin. She had had a great week and did not want it to end with her dealing with this lame situation, she thought to herself.

"Where your lame ass come from, I thought we been got rid of the trash. That's why you can't feed a stray dog; they always come back and find you," she said, loud enough for him to hear. She was already ready to buck the fuck up in this bitch she didn't mind going to jail tonight.

Marquise looked over at Maeve, mugging. Stating to himself, this bitch always has something to say. She knows I don't like her ass and when the fuck did, they start kicking it again. I thought I had gotten rid of this bitch for good. "Maeve, please mind ya business. I have no idea why she's hanging with you anyway, nothing but a hoe."

Leilani shook her head, her eyes never leaving Marquise's cold gaze. "No, I got this," she said softly, more to herself than to Maeve.

Marquise took a few steps toward their table, his expression unreadable but carrying a certain arrogance. "I didn't think I'd see you here tonight. Are we celebrating, and you forgot to invite me again? Have you been avoiding me, Leilani?"

Leilani's chest tightened, but she kept her posture steady, not giving him the satisfaction of showing vulnerability. "I'm not avoiding you, Marquise. I don't have time for whatever game you're trying to play. I have told you I'm done and want nothing to do with you. Where are your wife and kids? It's too late for a father to be out, especially when you've got a newborn, right?"

Ava looked at both Maeve and Leilani. She could tell there was deep tension, but no one had ever mentioned a Marquise. I can see why she thought to herself.

Maeve exchanged looks with Leilani, letting her know she could get popping in this bitch. However, she wanted to let her handle it because it would suit her growth. For some reason, Leilani looked stronger and tired of his bullshit. Maeve was used to Leilani folding every time this lame as nigga came around. Some things have changed, she thought.

Marquise smirked, leaning in a little too close for comfort. "You don't need to play the strong woman in front of your friends, Leilani. You know I can give you what you need. You have to stop fighting it." His voice lowered, dripping with condescension. He ignored the comment on his wife and kids, which is not helping their situation.

Leilani stood up slowly, meeting his eyes with unwavering strength. "I'm not playing around, and I don't want to keep repeating myself for some reason you are not understanding, Marquise. And for the record, I'm not interested in whatever you're offering anymore. Why won't you get it if you see me keep it moving, we don't have nothing to talk about."

She looked over to her cousin and Ava, who were now watching the scene unfold with concern. The tension was palpable.

I'm trying to move on and start over with my life. You should think about doing the same thing. So, move on with your family and help raise those kids. I am free and want to move that way; I will no longer be taking care of a whole family." She gave him a pointed glance. "I am currently dating someone now. Chemistry and I are taking it slow, with the end plan being for us to be together. He supports me, he never asks me for money or takes advantage of my time."

For a split second, Marquise's face faltered, but it was quick, like the flicker of a candle before it was smothered. He tried to mask his annoyance with a chuckle, but it didn't reach his eyes.

"Chemistry, huh?" He tilted his head, as though testing the sound of the words. "He sounds like a nice guy, but do you think this will last. You're out here saying you're dating. What grown ass woman talks like that either he ya man or he's not.

You think you're happy now, but things will change. You'll see. We always end up back where we started. This is merely a repetition of the past. You will let me know once you're ready again."

Leilani's jaw tightened, and she stood a little taller. "Well, not this time. Grown-ass adults with a purpose date one another—just two people. Not a hidden wife or hidden kids. You wouldn't know anything about that because when was the last time you took me out on a date? All you have done is take and take and take."

"You can't take it now that I have someone who sees an equal future for us. That's not my problem, and I don't owe you any explanations. I'm here to enjoy my night if you don't mind." Her voice was firm, confident—a voice that made it clear she was done with him.

Maeve stood back up again, sliding a protective arm around Leilani. "You heard the lady. Now, I think it's time for you to go. This isn't your place, and neither is she."

Marquise smirked since he was not paying attention to what Maeve was spitting. That lame ass bitch will never get a rise out of me. He gave a short nod, as if acknowledging her strength, but his words were sharp as he turned to leave.

"Fine. Enjoy your little night out, Leilani. But don't think for a second that this is over. I won't give up on you or us; it's better when we're together. You'll come back around... You always do."

Leilani didn't respond. She watched as Marquise and his friend made their way to the door, the tension between them still heavy.

When the door swung closed behind them, the atmosphere in the bar lightened, and Leilani let out a slow breath she didn't realize she'd been holding.

**

Ava was the first to speak, her voice full of concern but tinged with sympathy. "Are you okay, Leilani? Not gonna lie, you handled that situation like a classy bossy chick."

Leilani nodded, her heart still pounding, but her head was clear. "I'm fine. I've dealt with him before. He's just trying to get a rise out of me. Thank you for saying that I have come a long way. If you had seen me a couple of months ago, I would have left you both in the bar for that man. Oh, how the times have changed." She laughed!

Maeve grinned, clinking her glass with Leilani's. "Well, he's not gonna win tonight. And Ava is right, you handled that like a true classy chick. I am enjoying your glow-up. I never thought I would see the day you put that lame in his place. He is not on your side, nor does he have your best interests at heart. And I have been tired of him stealing your light over the years. You deserve someone better, and the way you brought up this Chemistry guy, I would love to meet him. Got my cousin bossing up."

Leilani smiled, finally feeling her shoulders relax. "Thank you both," she said quietly. "It feels good to be with people who have my back. And don't worry, you will be meeting him soon. He is such a breath of fresh air and so supportive." She smiled, thinking of him.

Ava gave her a warm smile. "I will always be there for you. You have been so inspirational to me in such a short time. You are stuck with me; you can do nothing about that."

With Marquise gone, they quickly fell back into their earlier rhythm. The music played, their drinks refilled, and laughter filled the air again. Leilani might've been shaken for a moment, but with her friend and cousin beside her, she knew she could handle whatever else life threw her way.

The night was still young, and this time, it was hers. He would not ruin her night; she is now making good memories.

"Hey, Leilani. I wanted to tell you how things are going at the job." Stated Ava

"Hell, yeah, now you know I want the tea, tell me what's going on with Mr. Hardling. Is he still trying to strong-arm you? And is he still trying to take credit for work done by others?" Leilani laughed.

"Oh, girl it has been a whole shit show. Tell me why he has been trying to get me to do extra work so he can appear more competent. Mr. Taylor is over him and the antics he tries to do in the office. This week alone, Mr. Hardling called HR and informed them that he believes Mr. Taylor is too involved in a position he doesn't manage. Oh, when Mr. Taylor found out it was hell to pay." She looked at Leilani and Maeve with wide eyes.

"Wait, is this the man's work you've been doing for years, Leilani? If so, he sounds lame as hell how the fuck has, he kept that job for so long," asked Maeve.

"Girl, yes, and he keeps his job because he likes to take all the credit for my work. I bet he is getting a run for his money messing around with Ava. She doesn't play no games with that man or take any of his shit." She laughed.

"Hell, naw, I don't, and he's still trying me. That's why he had to call HR, because I include Mr. Taylor in everything. Mr. Taylor instructed me to keep him included in everything. He said that he is working on some changes right now. They could come into effect as early as next month." Stated Ava.

"What kind of changes oh hell naw what the fuck has Mr. Hardling done now. He can never leave well enough alone. How do you keep going against one of the executives that man is sick in the head?" Leilani looked perplexed.

"I don't know now, but I will keep you updated. For some reason, I feel that the change will be both significant and loud. I'm here for it. Mr. Hardling needs to be taken down a notch, " said Ava.

Maeve signed loudly. "He sounds like a piece of work I hope the changes humble that ass. I would have been fired multiple times over fucking around with him. Don't nobody got time for that shit I would be committing crimes."

Both Ava and Leilani laughed at Maeve's sassiness. They both realize that she does not play any games and is not afraid to go there. You need a girl like Maeve on your team. Her turn-up is quick and no-nonsense.

Later, as the bar started to clear out, the three women stepped outside into the smoke garden. The cool air hit their faces, refreshing after the warmth inside.

"So," Maeve said with a mischievous smile, "I think it's time for a *proper* toast. To surviving the first week! And not allowing that lame Marquise to speak," she laughed!

Leilani grinned, lifting her glass. "To new beginnings and getting rid of old trash."

Ava raised her glass as well. "Yassss I love both toasts let's get it!"

The three clinked their glasses together, a moment of unity and strength. Leilani had no idea what the future held, but at that moment, surrounded by people who cared about her, she felt a sense of peace.

It was just the beginning, but it felt like everything was falling into place. She was now ready for her date with Chemistry. She enjoyed going out with him, and the dates kept her on a high.

Later that night, Leilani was sitting alone in her apartment. She stood by the window, watching the city lights blink like slow, lazy fireflies. The room was quiet, except for the refrigerator's hum and the distant rumble of a bus rolling down the avenue.

Once, the sound of a bus would have sent her heart into a tailspin — memories of cold vinyl seats and the suffocating fear of being left behind.

Now, she just watched it pass.

She wasn't the girl on the bus anymore.

She had built a shaky, messy, unfinished life, but it was hers. A life where people knew her name. Where promises didn't always end in goodbyes.

Her reflection caught in the glass, layered over the street beyond — older, braver, carrying every scar like a stitched seam on a worn backpack.

She smiled at her reflection. Not wide, not perfect. Just enough.

Maybe that was all she needed.

*

The Rooftop Showdown

It was the next night, and Leilani was so excited to see Chemistry. She had no idea how this man gave her butterflies each time she saw him. He is such a strong and protective man, and this was something she was not used to. For some reason, she was waiting for him to change into another Marquise.

However, she would be heartbroken if he became like Marquise. She also does not want the feeling of being seen to go away. It has been the best feeling ever, and someone wonderful is the cause of it.

The night air was crisp, the city skyline glowing with the soft hum of lights. The rooftop lounge was packed, but it felt intimate—the music was low, the drinks were strong, and the view stretched for miles.

Leilani sat across from Chemistry, feeling lighter than she had in years. She wore skinny jeans and a yellow, one-shoulder, sleeveless top. As usual, she likes to be off the floor in some cute and fun shoes, so she was wearing some yellow wedges with black straps, no toes out, but very flirtatious.

Chemistry looked very sexy in casual black jeans and a nice Timberland sweater. Of course, he finished his look with some wheat Timberland boots and some light jewelry.

"You did it, Lani," Chemistry said, leaning back in his seat. "First week down, and you ain't just keeping up with other people who have been there before you. You killed that shit but I had no doubts."

She smiled, warmth spreading through her chest. "It's been a long time since I've been this proud of myself. I started this job off strong, and it's going so well. I can't believe I left that old job behind to be included in such amazing projects."

Chemistry smirked. "Get used to it. I told you—you're built for this. You the shit for this job my smart baby. Give it a minute, you'll be one of the project managers, watch what I tell you!"

Just as she was about to respond, something shifted in the atmosphere.

That eerie, skin-prickling feeling—the kind that made the hairs on her neck stand up.

She was being watched.

Her eyes scanned the crowd, and then... *she saw him.*

Marquise. *Damn, here we go again. Why is this motherfucker everywhere I go? She thought. Maybe he will stay his simple ass over there with his wife.*

*

Sitting at a table in the back with his wife. Her back was facing me but his lame ass was all in my face.

He wasn't even focused on his wife in front of him. No, his entire body was turned toward *Leilani*. Eyes locked. Unblinking.

His wife was talking and smiling, her perfectly manicured hands gesturing as she spoke. But Marquise wasn't hearing a word she said.

He was watching Leilani **and studying her.**

And when his eyes flicked to Chemistry sitting across from her? The storm inside him cracked wide open. *Damn near every time I see her, she with this lame as nigga.*

Leilani's stomach twisted. *At this point he a fucking bug they need to stay they ass in the house. He didn't go out this damn much when we were together all them years.*

She turned back to Chemistry, trying to keep her composure. But it was too late—he had already noticed.

"I can see your body language smart baby please don't tell me this lame is somewhere in this motherfucker?" Chemistry asked, his tone sharp.

Before she could answer, Marquise was already up, headed toward them with a look that irritated the fuck out of her.

"Leilani," Marquise said, his voice loud, intense.

Chemistry stood immediately, squaring his shoulders. "Can I help you with something bro the fuck you over here in my girl face for?"

Marquise ignored him. He only had eyes for her.

"So, you have not considered anything we discussed last time I saw you?" Marquise asked, shaking his head like he couldn't understand. "You just gone keep playing with a nigga heart over someone you just met? I have been giving you space, but you need to get rid of him."

Leilani's throat tightened while Chemistry looked at her, trying to confirm what he was talking about. He would address that later; he would not be questioning her in front of this clown.

"Get rid of me?" Chemistry scoffed. "The only thing we need to be rid of is a begging ass dude that doesn't understand when a woman is done. If she wanted you, bruh, she would contact you. Now tell me how many calls have you received from her?"

Marquise *finally* looked at Chemistry, and his jaw tightened. "Man stay out of this shit. This is between me and my girl right here."

"See, that's your problem right there," Chemistry said, stepping closer. "You still think this beautiful woman belongs to you. Well, I don't know if you notice she done moved the fuck on."

"She's *mine and will always be mine no matter what*," Marquise growled. "You don't know what we've been through or what we had, you just entered the picture thinking you know her. She is mines and I know her inside and out that's what the fuck you don't understand."

"What you had is over move the fuck around quit harassing this woman before I fuck around and beat yo ass," Chemistry interrupted, "I am tired of repeating myself I'm not gone do too much more talking."

Marquise's nostrils flared, his fists clenching. "You don't know what you're talking about. And I'm not worried about your empty threat that shit don't move me."

Chemistry laughed, but there was no humor in it. "I know *exactly* what I'm talking about." His voice dropped lower, taking on a more menacing tone. "I know she was payin' your bills while you were layin' up with your wife. I know you've been playing both sides. And I know—" He leaned in. "—*she ain't yours anymore.*"

Marquise tensed; his entire body coiled like he was ready to explode.

"Why are you doing this, Leilani? And you telling him our business he doesn't have anything to do with our shit. He doesn't need to be anywhere in our shit we're working through complications right now." Marquise turned back to her; his voice was softer now. Pleading. "We belong together. You *know* that. Why won't you give me another chance, like you always have? I can be better to you, baby."

Leilani clenched her fists, her mind racing. She remembered a time when she had wanted him to talk to her like this. Beg her not to leave, as if she were the only woman in the world. But now it's different; he has a family, and I can no longer stay. I'm done being scared to be alone or unloved. If that is the way my life must end, I will accept it, but I will no longer take care of this man and his family.

For years, she had let him control the narrative. Let him define what they were. Let him convince her that she wasn't worth more. I let him dim my light for many years because I feared being left alone.

But *not anymore; I don't need anyone to make me feel important. Chemistry said I have all I need inside me, and I believe it.*

She exhaled sharply, lifted her chin, and said the words that finally set her free:

"Marquise, listen to me this last time. This man and I have decided to be together. And we will continue to be together until he or I decide it's done. You have no more influence over my life. I am moving on, whether you like it or not. I have nothing else to say to you about it."

Marquise froze.

"You heard what my girl said," Chemistry said, his voice unwavering. "Now back the fuck up before I *make* you."

The tension snapped. Marquise *lunged*.

Chemistry started beating his ass without hesitation. He was landing hits to his face and stomach. Soon enough, Marquise fell on a table, making it topple over to the ground. Marquise wasn't a fighter, so he wasn't a fair match for Chemistry. None of his punches were landing on Chemistry.

After the scuffle broke out, you could see the chairs thrown from the tables. You could also see the glass shatter all over the floor. Most of the people had already scrambled out of the way.

Marquise wanted *Leilani all for himself, like it's always been*. And at that moment, his brain was cloudy, with only thoughts of winning her over.

Again, like Deja vu, security rushed in, grabbing both men and separating them. The lounge was in chaos—people whispering, phones out recording.

Marquise thrashed against security's grip, his wild eyes locked on Leilani. "This isn't over," he shouted. "You *know* this ain't over! You know I will stop at nothing to get you back."

Leilani was getting tired of him and all the pop-ups. Like how the fuck is this nigga everywhere I go. In a minute, Chem is going to do something to him. I can feel that he is holding back because of me.

She was nervous looking over at Chemistry. He was still looking like he wanted to go beat him up again. I just met him and don't want to get him in trouble. But if there's one thing for sure, Leilani knew that Marquise would not stop until somebody got hurt.

Leilani sat stiffly in Chemistry's car's passenger seat, staring out the window but not seeing anything.

She could not understand how to get through Marquise thick fucking skull. We have been together for some years, but it's over. It's bizarre now that the tables have turned. A month ago, I would have had to beg, buy, and persuade him to stay. All he did was take; I was right there to make sure no stone was left overturned.

She could still hear Marquise's voice—his desperation, his anger. *This isn't over.*

But what he didn't understand is that I have grown. I have my own set of friends and family. I don't need to hold on to something unhealthy just because I want to be seen. Where has that gotten me over the years?

She swallowed hard, placing her hands on her thighs so she wouldn't tap her foot. *It was over, and I feel it has to be in my heart. This shit is no longer healthy and he's keeping me down. I want nothing to do with breaking up a family; my hands are clean, and I need to walk away that way.*

She did feel like he had some hold on her. *Why do I feel bad that he's hurting right now? Why do I think I need to do something to make him happy? Is it that I need closure? She thought.*

Beside her, Chemistry gripped the steering wheel, his jaw tight. He hadn't said much since they left the rooftop.

She knew he was letting her process and letting her breathe.

But the silence was suffocating.

"I should've known," she finally whispered.

Chemistry glanced at her. "Known what?"

She let out a bitter laugh. "That he'd never let me go. It was mostly about the money and the convenience. What he misses is having access to my time and money. He wants a mother, and he wants to continue to play that role. He needs me, but unfortunately, I don't need him anymore."

Chemistry scoffed. "Yeah, that happens when you feed a parasite for too long. They think they have the right to your blood."

Leilani exhaled, squeezing her eyes shut.

She turned to Chemistry, her voice raw. "What the hell am I going to do to make him leave me alone. And I saw you looking at me when he said he saw me. I went out with my cousin Maeve and Ava. His weird ass was in the bar and spotted me. He couldn't help but come over and say something. I told him yesterday that you and I are together. Maybe that's why he took it there tonight."

He sighed and ran a hand over his beard. "Oh, you don't have to worry bout him leaving you alone, believe that. I tried to stay out of yall shit but this lame as nigga keep testing me. And in a minute, I'm going to find out if he can pass that test. He's just holding on because you loved him, Lani. And because he made you believe he loved you too."

Her chest clenched.

She didn't want to admit it.

Didn't want to acknowledge that some part of her had been waiting—hoping—for Marquise to see her finally. *To finally choose her.*

"But he was too late and had too many people on his plate. Shit not to laugh, but I thought I was taking care of one person, not a whole family. She let out a sharp breath. "Man, I feel so stupid for allowing this to continue for so long."

Chemistry reached over and grabbed her hand in his. "Nah. Don't do that. It's not your fault; you loved and supported someone who took advantage of you. It was all nice when he could take your money and bring it to his family home. Think about it, baby. You've been taking the bus while he's driving around in his shit. You've been taking the bus for far too long. He was just a bum using a hard-working woman and her resources."

She looked up at him, eyes glossy.

"You weren't stupid," he said firmly. "You were *loyal*. You were *giving*. You were everything he didn't deserve. *That's not on you. It's a lot of loyal people who don't understand they are being taken for a ride. Things finally snap into place when you're so low or see the person for who they are.*"

She stared at him, her throat tightening.

He wasn't just saying words.

He *meant* them.

For the first time in years, she felt *seen*.

But before she could respond, a sharp *buzz* from her phone broke the moment.

She glanced down.

Marquise.

How is this motherfucker sending text messages to me where the fuck is his wife. This shit is getting on my nerves now. She went ahead and blocked his ass there was no way he was on her line after all this.

She flipped the phone over, facedown.

Chemistry was watching her. "You want me to block his ass for you?"

She huffed a short laugh, shaking her head. "You don't have to worry about that, Chem. I have already blocked his ass. I'm getting a headache now, and it doesn't make sense that he's already blowing up my phone. Man, he needs to chill the fuck out it has already been a long night"

Chemistry was happy to hear her say this. He is not going to lie; she is making him somewhat nervous. It would hurt him to find out that she has not truly moved on. I don't understand how a lame as nigga can have such a hold on such a beautiful soul.

**

Marquise sat in the driver's seat of his car, gripping the steering wheel so tight his knuckles were white.

His wife sat in the passenger seat beside him, arms crossed, lips pursed.

The silence was suffocating.

Then finally—

"You made a damn fool of yourself tonight. How you up in that bitch fighting and they had all them cell phones out. What about our image, Marquise? How does it look to you, fighting another man when you've got a wife? Our numbers are climbing right now, but it seems like you couldn't care less."

His jaw clenched. "Leave it alone, Monica. I'm not thinking about social media likes and comments right now. My damn eye is swollen and my mouth is leaking but all you want to talk about is some dame likes and comments."

She laughed. A sharp, bitter sound. "Leave it alone? *Leave it alone?* Oh, you mean like how you left me sitting there, looking crazy, while you chased after *her*? And you damn right I don't care that you got ya ass beat anit nobody tell you to go over there. Once that man stepped up, you should have stopped and moved around. You don't know what's going on with that girl. If she fucking with you a married man who's to say she not fucking with a criminal. I mean damn I don't even recognize you right now. Just fucking our shit up knowing how long it took us to get here."

Marquise didn't respond.

Monica turned toward him, her eyes flashing. "Tell me, Marquise—how long has this been going on? How long have you been in *love* with her? I have never seen you respond like this over a woman. Tell me the truth, Marquise," she yelled!

Marquise flinched.

He wasn't in love with Leilani.

Was he? He never even thought about love when it came to her. He knew she was always there for him, no matter what. She would do anything to make sure he was good. That was as far as he believed his feelings went. Now he wasn't so sure.

"She was just—" He swallowed, shaking his head. "She was just somebody who helped me out."

Monica scoffed. "*Helped you out*? Are you serious? That's all you got to tell me?"

"I mean it wasn't—"

"It wasn't *what*?" she snapped. "It wasn't cheating? It wasn't real? Because from where I was sitting, it sure as hell looked real when you got up like a damn lunatic and ran after her. Every time I turn around you in this bitch face. But you want to sit here and tell me she was just somebody who helped you."

Marquise clenched his jaw, his mind racing.

He had never thought about it before. He never really took the time to think about what Leilani meant to him.

She had always just... *been there.*

Loving him

Supporting him

Taking care of him.

She never needed the attention like Monica did. Never needed the validation of strangers on social media.

She was quiet. Steady. **His.**

And now she was gone.

Monica exhaled sharply and turned back to the window. "You're pathetic sitting acting like she doesn't mean anything to you. Hell, even a blind man can tell something is going on there."

His grip on the wheel tightened. "Don't start, Monica. Wont you leave the shit alone already? Its aint enough I got my ass beat and you worried about the wrong thing."

She shook her head, laughing under her breath. "You know what? I should've known why you keep trying to change the damn subject."

"Known what?"

"That you weren't done with her," she said. "I saw how you looked at her at the lounge. I *felt* it. You don't look at me like that, and I gave you three kids. Where is your love for me, Marquise?"

Marquise pressed his lips together.

She wasn't wrong.

Monica stared out of the window, her voice quieter now. "You know what's funny? I wasn't even worried about the other women. The random bitches you be running around town with. I felt like you were being a man, having some fun. I *knew* they meant nothing to you because you had us." She turned back to him, her eyes sharp. "But oh, how the tables have turned because despite what you say, I know you love her. I've noticed you don't even get up with these hoes anymore. I should have said something when I saw that."

Marquise swallowed hard.

"Be real, Marquise. If she had let you? You would've *left me* for her. You would have ended our family, everything we have worked so hard for. You would throw everything away?"

He didn't answer.

Because they both already knew the truth.

And for the first time, it hit him—

Maybe he did love her. And now was the right time to let her know how much. He would give her some time, but not let her go. There is no way I would let her be with this thug ass nigga. He does not fit my classy baby.

*

Moving On

The next morning, Leilani was hard at work. Simone has many projects underway simultaneously. Leilani was eagerly keeping up with all the super-fast moments. She did not have time to talk to her team members.

She was too busy checking all the locations set for the city's various planning projects. She confirmed that all the catering companies were in place, and if the event required music, she booked artists from the approved lists.

She was knee deep in her research for the next city event, which includes different mayors within a 100-mile radius who meet every two years. Simone did say that this time of year was busy, and don't worry about the rush. For some reason, Leilani felt right at home with the fast-paced environment.

"Leilani," Simone called out to her.
"Yes, Simone, I'm so sorry. I was deep into researching new things for the next event. Leilani looked up from her desktop screen.

"Don't worry about it, Leilani," she said, chuckling. "Can you please sit in at Zephyr's next meeting. He has requested that you help out in his area."

"Wait," Caius said, "I usually help him the most with the events he works. Leilani would have a big learning curve trying to step in at this time of the year." He looked worried.

"Everything will be fine, Caius. He also wants everyone to attend the meeting this afternoon. Leilani has several proposals, so I would like her to present them to Zephyr. I would rather Leilani Walk through her examples; no reason for me to do so. She is strong, and I want to get her in front of this. So, can you all report to room EC4D in about 15 minutes?" And with that, Simone smiled as a matter of fact and walked off from the group.

Caius, Aurelius, and Lorelei looked over at Leilani. Caius had a salty look on his face. Lorelei rolled her eyes while Aurelius smirked, and then she looked over at Caius.

"All of this is fine, I get it, they want the strongest person to get the new person up to speed. I can do that, no problem, Leilani, we've got this!" Caius said. "I am going to the restroom before we start our meeting. He hurriedly ran off without another word.

"So, you know, they ask all of us to run our ideas by them. So, this is no big deal. I'm going to get a snack since we won't be able to have lunch. I know this meeting is going to run over. I will be back before the meeting. Lorelei stated what an attitude.

"Damn, I've made a couple of people mad, and I have not done my shit yet! I have not shown my ass just yet; these people want me. There is no way I'm not going to show the fuck out!" Leilani laughed.

"No, for real, cause NO, they do not let us show them our ideas. Caius has tried since I have been here." He laughed. "They're both just hating because if we are being honest, this has never happened. Whatever you put together, I guarantee you that all six project managers have already seen it and had a discussion. They arrive at the office around 5 am. Like they legit be in this motherfucker at that time no lie." Aurelius said.

"Oh, damn I knew it was something cause Caius looked like he wanted to say so much more but Simone shut that ass down. Seems like she was trying to make him feel better about the situation, in my opinion. Plus, what is up with ol' girl? I have done nothing to her, and she just isn't feeling my vibe." Leilani asked, looking confused.

"Oh, sis you not special she just a bitch at all times. I think they are keeping her until they find someone to replace her. No one knew you were coming until you arrived. But many of the managers are tired of her, too, you can tell. Also, they all don't work with her that much anyway; she seems like she's just an extra body." Aurelius said with confidence.

"Man, that crazy she got all that negative energy. And I did nothing out of the ordinary. This is the same activity I did at my old job. I always look at the current project, analyze the budget, and ensure it aligns with expectations. Sometimes that leads me to find better opportunities or remove an oddly over-budget project." Leilani said with ease.

"Damn sis you cold, you got the brains I see why they snatch yo ass up!" Aurelius said, laughing.

Before Leilani could respond, Caius returned and asked if everybody was ready to head over. She nodded yes, and Aurelius got up and straightened his suit and tie. Lorelei came over, munching on something as they were about to walk off. It was not as if they could tell because she had gobbled it up so quickly; they all wondered if she had taken a breath.

Leilani was set to be the last person to enter the room, but Aurellius made sure to walk into the room behind her. Leilan froze in her tracks when she noticed all the project managers were in attendance. They were already sitting at the huge round table.

"Hi guys, please sit, and we can get started. Thanks for joining us this afternoon," Elio said with a big grin.

Everyone smiled and found a seat scared shitless. They didn't tell Leilani that this was new and out of the ordinary. I swear this man always has a grin on his face. I don't know if it's creepy or if he is delighted, Leilani thought.

"So, to first break the ice," Ozias stated, "No one is in trouble. We want to keep you all informed of any changes. As you are aware, we have six project managers who must share four interns. This has worked, but we want to make a more permanent solution."

Everyone looked on, perplexed. Leilani thought, "I just got here. What the hell is the change so quickly?" She was nervous. Was this something she did? But they just said no one was in trouble. Leilani, stop it, she thought.

Starting next week, you all will be company employees with the title of event coordinator. Of course, your pay will be increased, and this job is now full-time. Our business has picked up, and we want a solid team behind us and all the work we have coming." Said Ozias.

Everyone started to loosen up and smile. Caius was thrilled because he felt he had finally gotten what he wanted. The environment shifted, and the air became lighter.

"When you all return to your desks, there is a new file on your desk tops. Please make sure you are familiar with the latest information and responsibilities. Additionally, please confirm that no personnel files are stored on your desktops. When you come back on Monday, each of you will have a new laptop. We need you ready to move, and some traveling may come up shortly. Ozias smiled.

"Now that is all for today, please return to your desk until the end of the day." Said Ozias.

They all got up to leave the room when Leilani reached the door to cross the threshold. She heard her name being called.

"Oh, Leilani," asked Simone. "Can you please stay for a moment? I still want you to go over the ideas you submitted."

"Yes, of course I have all my notes here with me," Leliani said.

Leliani spent the next 55 minutes reviewing all of her analysis. She also explained her reasoning for eliminating some events while keeping others. Simone had already put together a PowerPoint and stated that she had made it, so explaining each area to each manager was far too easy.

Once she was done, she felt like all the air had left her body. She had been talking for so long that she had not realized the team had been taking notes.

"That was such great information, Leilani. When you put this information together, I was so impressed, having only been here for four weeks. I knew we had to have a conversation with all the leaders. And they all agree with how impressive you have been. We understand that you have not been here long. But what we are proposing, we all agree you can handle." Simone said with a smile.

However, Leilani was super nervous. Were they going to tell her that she was fired? What were they going to say to her? Does this company no longer need me? What is happening here? I have ruined my chances because I always give too much initially. I knew I should have just kept quiet like I always do; it's so much safer. Damn, I messed up, she thought.

"Leilani," Simone repeated her name.

Leilani had no idea how many times she had called her name.

"Oh, I'm sorry, Simone, what did you say?" Ask Leilani.

"We want you to be the leader of the other three, with a possible four, as we would need to replace you. I know this is a shock because you've just joined the team. But you have helped so much that it would only be right if you managed everyone."

"That way, you can make a plan and have each coordinator execute while focusing on high-level things. Now this is something to think about over the weekend. Don't answer now. Let's talk more on Monday. I know this was a lot, and you probably want to escape from us." She laughs.

Leilani was lost and didn't know how to respond, so she stared blankly.

"Leilani," Iris said. "We see you."

"Yes," Allegra followed up. "It's a lot to take in, like Simone said. Just think about it; no words are needed now. Go ahead and return to your desk. As all of your colleagues have left, please go home for the day. We will talk more on Monday. Have a great weekend."

Leilani had nothing more to say. She shook her head and hurriedly left the room, with numerous thoughts on her mind.

And true to their word, everyone was already gone, so she did not have to explain everything. **GOOD,** she thought!

She looked down at her phone and saw a text from her brother Aurelius.

"I know you got tea. I tried to wait, but you were taking forever. Make sure you hit me up this weekend. Now you know I'm in everybody's business lol. Have a great weekend, lil sis.

Leilani smiled. I will reach out to him later this weekend.

**

Leilani stepped out of her office building, her body buzzing with a mix of exhaustion and satisfaction. The first four weeks of her internship as the event coordinator had been *intense*, but she was holding her own. Obviously, because they want me to lead a whole team, and I just got here.

Her mind drifted to the weekend. Chemistry had already texted her, asking if she wanted to do something this weekend after the madness at the rooftop.

And for once?

She was looking forward to it.

But just as she pulled out her phone to check the time, a sleek black car pulled up to the curb in front of her.

Her stomach dropped.

The window rolled down, and there he was.

Marquise.

His eyes locked onto hers, and for a second, neither moved.

Then he stepped out.

Leilani's breath hitched.

He looked... *different*.

Disheveled. Tired. His usual cocky smirk was nowhere to be found.

"Lani," he said, his voice low, desperate. "Can we talk? Please, can you give me a moment?"

Her fingers tightened around her phone. "I have nothing to say to you, Marquise. I have no conversation to give you, Marquise."

He exhaled, rubbing a hand over his head. "Please. Just five minutes. I will make this as fast as possible."

She stared at him.

A part of her wanted to walk away, to keep moving like he didn't exist. But another part that had spent *years* loving him needed to hear whatever excuse he was about to spit out.

With a sharp inhale, she crossed her arms. "Five minutes."

Marquise's shoulders relaxed like he had just won the lottery.

He leaned against the car. "I messed up."

Leilani scoffed. "Which time?"

His lips pressed together, and for once, he didn't have a slick comeback.

"I was wrong about everything," he admitted. "I took you for granted. I didn't appreciate what you did for me, what you *mean* to me."

She clenched her jaw, waiting.

"I let my pride get in the way," he continued. "But you're the only woman who ever *saw* me, Lani. You never needed the attention, the validation. You just *loved* me." He swallowed, stepping closer. "I miss you. And I know I don't deserve another chance, but I swear, I'll make it right if you let me. I love you, Leilani."

Leilani let out a slow breath.

Once upon a time, those words would have made her melt in his arms. It was what she always wanted to hear from him. Once upon a time, she would have let herself believe him.

But now?

Now, all she felt was *tired*. His love no longer mattered; she had moved on to someone who treated her better and didn't keep secrets.

She tilted her head. "And what about your wife and kids, does she know about your lover for me?"

Something flickered in his eyes. "Monica knows how I feel about you, and my kids are going to be straight no matter where my heart lies."

She gave a bitter laugh. "Marquise, you can't be fucking serious right now. What kind of man would leave a woman with three kids? One of them happens to be a newborn baby. That shit so disgusting."

Marquise flinched. He didn't recognize this version of Leilani standing before him.

Leilani shook her head. "You only want me now because I finally walked away. Because you can't stand the idea of me with someone else."

His jaw clenched. "Is it *him*? Chemistry? That dude you were with?" Ignoring the comments about him making his wife a single mother. He didn't give a fuck he was tired of Monica anyway. If he could take his kids from her and be with Leilani, that would be the perfect ending.

Her eyes narrowed. "It doesn't matter."

Marquise's face twisted. "So that's it? You're just *done*?"

Leilani exhaled, something inside of her settling. "Yes."

His hands curled into fists. "Lani—"

"No," she said, her voice firm. "You don't get to do this. You don't get to try and drag me back just because you finally realize what you lost." She shook her head. "You were never gonna leave your wife. You were never gonna change. You just liked knowing I'd always be there."

She stepped back, holding up her phone.

And right there, in front of him—

She blocked all his social media.

His face fell, because he didn't know she could see that information. She never made it seem like she had time to go online. He was hella stuck because this meant she had seen everything regarding my marriage. She had seen that happy image that he now regrets every day. What kills him the most is how he can't explain it's fake when it's in print, with likes and validations.

Leilani felt a strange lightness in her chest. This was it.

The final cut.

She turned on her heel and walked away, not bothering to look back.

**

As she walked away, her phone vibrated with a text.

From *Chemistry*.

"Still down for tonight? I'll pick you up at 8."

Leilani smiled.

And responded with a yes, accompanied by a kissy emoji. Leilani finally made it home from work, and she was worn out. That didn't matter, though, because she was about to see Chemistry later. She dropped her bags on the couch after she shut and locked the front door.

Walking back to the bathroom, she started taking off her clothes. Once she reached the bathroom, she threw the dirty clothes in the hamper. Looking at herself in the mirror, she smiled, reflecting on everything that had happened.

I have come a long way. Can you believe this all started when I did my boss, Mr. Hardling's, job while he took the credit? *There were days she wanted to take his ass outside* she laughed jokingly. Now she was at a new job, and they were asking her to lead the interns. Times have changed, she thought, as she adjusted the water temperature.

Once the water reached her desired temperature, she stepped into the shower and continued to think. I would have believed that Marquise and I would have been married by now. I never thought he would have a wife and some kids living it up somewhere. I still don't understand how I was that blind. Why did I not see what was going on?

The whole time, I just thought he was a cheater, possibly having a couple of women on the side who wanted to fight. Even that was me being delusional and accepting things so I wouldn't end up alone. What he was hiding, though, was much worse. I would never ruin a family; it's all I ever want in this world. I could see myself being a mother; I thought I would be a mother to Marquise's first child. Oh, how wrong I was.

After she washed her whole body twice, she stepped out of the shower and grabbed the towel. She then pats herself dry, starting with her arms and working her way down.

She was still pondering everything that had transpired. She was happy to have moved on from Marquise, but she would not lie to herself about it. She was also scared. What if I am alone forever? I mean, Chemistry could be with me because he enjoys saving someone. She thought he might go on his way once he was deemed the hero.

I mean, those are negative thoughts. I don't know what to expect from Chemistry yet. I want to give him a chance because he sees me. No one has ever seen me for who I am. If they did, however, they did not fully accept the real me. I will do my best to think and feel more positive. Negative thoughts seem to attract ass holes who are leaches. I don't know much about Chemistry, but that man is a breath of fresh air, and it helps that he has that hood swagger.

I am also happy to have my cousin Mae back in my life. I can't believe I let Marquise keep her away from me these past couple of years. My cousin works, and she is thinking about going back to school. The best part of her is that she loves me and supports me. I know she would never leave me, Leilani, though smiling.

And then there is Ava's sophisticated new bestie. Something about that girl screams classiness and professionalism. I love being around her, and I hope we can deepen our connection by getting to know one another.

Leilani is also happy to have met Aurelius. He has taken to her like a big brother, and she was sure that she was older. Lord knows she doesn't deal with her full-blooded siblings, as they've got their problems between them. However, she was interested in seeing where their sister-brother bond could go.

She finished by rubbing her entire body down with a mixture she had created. Nothing major, just cocoa butter lotion, Vaseline, and baby oil gel, to name a few of the ingredients.

After that, she pulled out some white jeans with tears running down the pant legs. Behind the areas with the tears, there was a soft, purple threading. She paired this with a silky purple blouse with white buttons from top to bottom. She wanted to wear some cute heels, but she settled for white boots that went up to her ankles.

She loved to wear boots with heels; it was her signature look. She finished her look by spraying on some of her favorite perfume. She felt beautiful and happy with the fit she picked out. Now, all she had to do was wait for Chemistry to pull up.

About ten minutes later, Chemistry texted her. She looked at the text, which read "outside." Leilani smiled and rushed to grab her leather jacket. She walked out the door and locked it with her key behind her.

Her boots clicked against the sidewalk like punctuation. With each step forward, a sentence in a new chapter, she was finally ready to write.

Across the street, Chemistry waited, leaning against his car. The streetlights cast soft gold across his face, and he smiled when he saw her coming.

This is the man I have chosen now, and if it doesn't work out, it will be okay. She is no longer interested in someone who tries to break her down. Her sights were set on someone who wanted to help her build herself up.

She reached him and slid into his arms without a word. For a moment, everything was quiet — a stillness she hadn't felt in years.

"Damn you smelling and looking good Leilani" Chemistry said while holding her firmly in their embrace. "I have missed you."

"I have missed you too, Chemistry, and you look damn good yourself," she laughed and kissed him on the lips.

Chemistry finally let her go and opened the passenger side door for her to step in. Once she was safely inside, he closed the door behind her and ran to the driver's side.

He got into the car and then hit the push start, and the car came alive. "I hope it's okay if we just head to the rooftop bar," he stated. Well, my rooftop bar, but we will get to that later.

"Of course, that sounds fun, you know I love that bar. I can believe it's your bar, it fits your vibe. Plus, they make the best drinks them shits don't be all water down so I been notice something" she winked and smiled.

At that moment, she laughed again, thinking about the fun she would have tonight, and a text came through.

For some reason, Marquise's voice came to her mind. She could hear him saying that it did not matter what she said; they would be together. You will be back. You can't stand to be alone, and you know it, so take your time, baby.

It didn't matter anymore, though. We're done, she thought. This was final, and she felt as though a door quietly closed and locked behind her.

She glanced down and her phone unlocked. She clicked on a text from an unknown number.

The message read: **I'm on to you Bitch. Watch yo back, Leilani!**

Her smile turned upside down, and she locked the screen.

"What is it?" Chemistry asked, searching her face. He was now connected to her, and when her energy shifts, he can feel it.

Leilani looked ahead, her voice steady. "Why won't people just leave me alone? There is no reason for this shit."

She took a deep breath to calm down. "Now you know a moherfucka is hating when they sending shit from an unknown number? Never has an unknown number texted me. I don't have time for this shit. She said, frustrated.

"What the hell does the message say? Asked Chemistry.

"They sending this bullshit like watch my back. I don't bother anybody, and now people are threatening me. I swear this better not have nothing to do with Marquise ass. He will stop at nothing to win me back this shit is crazy." Leilani stared out the front windshield.

Chemistry looked over at her, looking confused and a bit irritated, not by her but by her situation." What's going on now? You can't just enjoy yourself; it's something every day." He was tired of dude fucking with her.

Before she could respond, her phone rang—

Another unknown number.

She hesitated, staring at the screen, growing increasingly annoyed with each passing second.

Whoever was on the other end of this call was about to get cussed the fuck out. All she wanted to do was enjoy her night this shit is ridiculous.

She answers.

A distorted voice crackles through the line.

"You think you're gonna get away with this shit, Leilani? You have no idea how I'm coming."

She couldn't get a word in because the person hung up quickly.

Chemistry looked at her with an angry expression on his face. "What the hell is that lame up to now. Don't tell me he's still bothering you?" I see I'm going to have to make time to visit him, **he thought with an evil smirk.**

She just sat there, confused. Who the hell would be threatening her? She is done messing around with Marquise. She only had two known enemies, but she was done with everything involving Marquise. They said I don't know how they're coming. What they don't know is I'm no longer "*The Girl on the Bus,* and I will no longer be unseen. She smiled proudly.

She used to think love was something you bought with silence and sacrifice. That if you gave enough, stayed long enough, bent far enough, you'd finally be chosen.

But now? She was done trying to earn what should've been given freely. She wanted to explore someone who reciprocated her love. She should not have to damage herself to uphold someone; that's not love.

Love would find her whole.

And if it didn't?

She still had herself.

For the first time in years, Leilani wasn't waiting to be picked.

She was picking herself.

*

Acknowledgments

I want to thank the bus monitor from the bus that day. She went above and beyond when she realized she had left a child behind. Her actions following that unfortunate event helped highlight the lifelong relationship between family and child.

I want to thank all the mothers around the world who do the best they can with the hand life has dealt them. Some mothers have to do it alone, with little to no assistance, and they still show up.

A special shoutout to all the real-life Chemistries out there: the men who want nothing more than to see women shine and find strength within themselves. They see us.

Thank you to the family members who don't give up. You may be annoying (yes, you), but believe me, we love you for it.

And thank you to anyone who has ever supported me on my journey. Standing out is hard. But being me? That's where I'm most comfortable.

*

About the author

E. Vale is a fiction writer and visual storyteller for children and anyone who still remembers what it felt like to be one. Her vivid imagination brings fictional worlds to life—worlds that celebrate strength, nurture growth, and gently explore how we handle conflict.

There's always more to discover memory, acceptance, and second chances.

She holds a degree in Civil Engineering and resides in the Midwest, where she balances spreadsheets during the day and tackles emotional battles at night.

Her debut novel, *The Girl on the Bus*, was born from a deep fascination with how childhood fears echo through adult lives—and how writing can become a tool for healing childhood wounds.

When she's not writing, she's probably sketching story scenes in Procreate, binge-watching true crime documentaries, or buying more notebooks than she'll ever fill.

Connect with her at **EValeStories.com** or on TikTok and Instagram **@E.ValeWrites**.

*

Let's Stay Connected

Thank you for reading *The Girl on the Bus*. If Leah's story moved you, captured your soul, or made you feel seen, I'd love to stay in touch.

Join my mailing list for updates on new releases, behind-the-scenes content, and exclusive extras from E. Vale.

EValeStories.com/newsletter

Follow me on social media for bookish fun, writing updates, and late-night thoughts about fictional characters and vending machine snacks:
TikTok & Instagram: @E.ValeWrites

Leave a review if you enjoyed the book! Reviews help readers find stories that matter—and every single one means the world.

Leave yours on Amazon, Goodreads, or wherever you share book love. **Want more?**

I'm currently working on new stories that dive even deeper into resilience, memory, and healing. Stay tuned—this ride isn't over yet.

With love and wild imagination, **E. Vale**

*